THE CHARABANC OF DEATH

A BELINDA LAWRENCE MYSTERY

I0659163

BRIAN KAVANAGH

VIVID
PUBLISHING

To discover more Brian Kavanagh books,
or to contact the author, please visit
www.vividpublishing.com.au/briankavanagh

Copyright © 2025 Brian Kavanagh

ISBN: 978-1-923078-94-9
Published by Vivid Publishing
A division of the Fontaine Publishing Group
P.O. Box 948 Fremantle
Western Australia 6959
www.vividpublishing.com.au

For the memory of dear friends who travelled part of the way with me.

"I write for myself and strangers. The strangers, dear Readers, are an afterthought."

— Gertrude Stein

ABOUT THE AUTHOR

Producer/Director/Editor/Writer

With many years experience in film production Brian Kavanagh's career covers the areas of Production, Direction, Editing and Writing on features and documentaries.

Kavanagh is an accredited member of the Australian Screen Editors (A.S.E) by which he was honoured with a Lifetime Achievement Award in 1997 for his contribution to film making in Australia.

He is also a member of the Australian Society of Authors (A.S.A.).

CHAPTER ONE

...the suspected immediate cause of death, as determined by the condition of the heart, suggests that the deceased likely suffered from tuberculosis complicated by...

The words flowed across the computer screen, a digital tapestry woven by a man whose fingers moved with practiced agility over the keyboard. His hands were long and lean, exuding an aura of maturity and sophistication, while his strong physique hinted at a man who took pride in his health and vitality. The gentle strains of a Chopin nocturne filled the room, its melodious notes battling against the undercurrent of urgency that permeated the air.

...it is possible there was another, yet unknown cause of death...

A Siamese cat, her striking blue eyes intently fixed on the rhythmic dance of her master's fingers, felt a stir of curiosity but hesitated to approach; she had learned from past experiences that her master could be quick to anger, and she did not want to provoke him. The man finished typing, pressed the "Read Aloud" button, and reclined back in his chair, listening to the robotic female voice recite his text—monotonous and devoid of emotion.

"It had been observed that the heart was shrouded in pale, white, stringy substances, accompanied by slight abrasions, suggesting tuberculosis complications. As previously stated, this

1

is by no means confirmed, and if further examination of the heart is permitted, it may unveil the true cause of death..."

As the voice echoed in the room, the man's thoughts drifted to a quote that danced tantalizingly at the edge of his mind. "Remember that wherever your heart is, there you will find your treasure." Ah yes... he recalled the author—Paulo... what was his last name?

The sterile voice interrupted his fleeting thoughts, prompting him to click the Print button. The sudden whir of the printer startled the cat, who watched with wide eyes as the blank page transformed into text, revealing the fruits of her master's labour. Before she could pounce on this unexpected prize, he deftly snatched the paper away, folded it carefully, and laid it on the desk beside a printed email that awaited his attention...

from: Jenny Forrest <JForrest@mailE.com>
to: Andre Levinz <LevinzA@mailE.com>
date: September 15th, 2:00 PM
subject: Booking Confirmation
Dear Mr. Levinz, This is to confirm your booking on a motor flight.

The computer, now closing, consumed the Nocturne leaving the room steeped in an almost eerie quiet. With a decisive snap, he closed his suitcase, the sound echoing in the stillness, and glanced at the watch on his wrist—its hands ticking away precious moments. It was time to leave. The early direct flights from Warsaw Chopin Airport to Paris had long since departed, and the remaining options were fully booked. Normally, he would have chosen the train, a leisurely ride that stretched over fourteen hours, but today's urgent business demanded speed. His only option was the City Hopper, a tedious journey that tortured him with an eight-hour travel time, including a frustrating stopover in Amsterdam, not to mention wildcat Union strikes. He gathered his suitcase and essential documents, allowing himself a fleeting touch of affection as he patted the cat on the head.

"The dozorca will take care of you as usual, Mazurka," he uttered, hurrying from the apartment. As the elevator doors closed with a dull thud, Mazurka perked up, her ears twitching at the sound of the mechanism descending to the street below. Stepping out onto Ulica Poloneza, Mr. Levinz blinked against the gentle autumn sunlight that bathed the street, a welcome warmth enveloping him. Checking his watch once more, he quickened his pace, urgency propelling him toward the taxi rank outside the nearby hotel, where he hoped a cab would be waiting to whisk him away to his next destination. As he did so a chance thought came to mind...Paulo Coelho, the author of the quote.

CHAPTER TWO

Jenny Forrest clicked off her mobile phone and set it down on the café table, its surface cool beneath her fingers. The early Parisian evening light cast long shadows as the sun dipped below the horizon. Faint stars began to emerge in the twilight sky, twinkling like gems, while the vibrant atmosphere of the Left Bank came alive with laughter and conversation. Diners filled the inviting outdoor terraces of their favorite restaurants, delighting in le chef d'œuvre du jour, and animatedly discussing the events of their day, making plans for the evening, and critiquing the rich, velvety wines that flowed freely.

Jenny savoured the last morsels of her creamy fromage, relishing the delicate flavours as she clicked on her tablet, eager to capture her thoughts in writing. The phone call she had just received was from a latecomer wanting to join the Motor Flight tour, a man named Andre Levinz calling from Amsterdam. His voice had crackled through the line with urgency, confirming his intent to join the excursion that was set to depart in the following days. This unexpected addition would bring the number of tourists to nine, a departure from the usual eight. She would need to arrange for extra bookings—accommodations and meals—tasked with the promise of a busy but manageable workload for the next day. Her introspection was briefly interrupted when the waiter approached with the bill, neatly placing it on the table. As he retreated, Jenny's thoughts drifted back to the peculiar phone call. Andre had sounded irritable, his words tumbling out in a rush, as if the very act of joining the tour was a matter of personal necessity. Jenny couldn't help but wonder what lay beneath his insistence; after all, the motor flight tour was merely a recreation of a nostalgic car journey undertaken by the illustrious writers Edith Wharton and Henry James through France in 1907. Yet, she had learned to navigate the diverse personalities of her tour groups, and she felt confident that she could handle the enigmatic Andre Levinz.

Rising, Jenny prepared to leave. As she made her way to the register, a few male patrons paused their conversations, captivated by the sight of this tall, elegant English woman in a fitted dark blue uniform that exuded a sense of professionalism and service. Unbeknownst to her, their admiration lingered in the air, but Jenny remained oblivious to their intrigued stares. Her mind was still engulfed in thoughts surrounding the unexpected tourist. The urgency in his voice echoing in her ears as she reached for her phone, ready to tackle the challenges that lay ahead.

CHAPTER THREE

As she drove away from her charming hillside cottage, ZeZe Dupont made a mental note to remind the gardener to prune the lavender when the coming winter came to a close. The crisp Normandy air filled her lungs as the evening light settled across the landscape. The winding drive to Paris would soon envelop her in the familiar embrace of her apartment on the Quai d'Orsay. Yet, the enchanting allure of Paris occupied none of her thoughts. Instead, ZeZe was consumed with anticipation. The coming weeks would reveal whether her meticulously crafted plans would bear fruit, but an unexpected complication had arisen, and she was determined to tackle it head-on. Too much time and effort had been invested in her audacious scheme for it to falter now. She had braced herself for resistance, but she was resolute in her mission, even if it meant vanquishing her rival. Her phone chimed, announcing a new message. With a swift glance from the road to the screen, she read the notification:

Monday 8:30 PM: Additional guest late booking: Andre Levinz. Jenny.

A sardonic smile formed on ZeZe's lips. She reached for a chocolate from the box nearby, a private celebration, her heart racing as she pressed her foot deeply into the accelerator. So, he had taken the bait. She navigated through the dimly lit, nearly deserted streets of Sourdeval, the echoes of her wheels reverberating against the quaint stone buildings. As she passed the cemetery, she noticed the grave diggers emerging from their grim duties, their expressions shadowed by the weight of their work. Yet, lost in her own turbulent thoughts, ZeZe hardly registered their presence. In a fleeting moment, her car crushed a forgotten floral wreath that had been left on the road—a crumpled remnant of love and remembrance, now squashed and devoid of meaning. It lay unrecognizable, a silent testament to those who had mourned. As the image faded in her rearview mirror, ZeZe steadied her gaze forward, resolved to confront whatever challenges lay ahead.

CHAPTER FOUR

Obadiah James cursed himself for not splurging on a few extra Euros to take a taxi from Charles de Gaulle Airport which would have whisked him directly into the heart of Paris. Instead, he found himself stuck on a painfully slow bus, inching through the relentless chaos of Parisian traffic. The cacophony of honking horns and chattering voices filled the air, startling him and pulling him from his thoughts. He leaned against the window and sighed, yearning for the serene familiarity of home on Main Street in Cashiers, North Carolina. There, the streets were quiet, and the only real traffic bottlenecks occurred on Sunday mornings as churchgoers filled the roads. In truth, with fewer than a thousand residents, Cashiers rarely saw anything that could be classified as heavy traffic.

As the bus crept along, a flash of impatience shot through him. He checked his watch again, noting that he only had half an hour to go before the daunting task of navigating to his hotel for a scheduled check in. The French language had eluded him; his attempts at mastering it were too sporadic and ultimately unsatisfactory. He chuckled to himself at the thought that only the French could manage to inject so much passion into grammar. How was anyone supposed to decipher whether a noun was male or female? Despite this frustration, he had memorized a handful of phrases that he hoped would be useful once he stepped off the bus. The travel agent had also provided him with detailed instructions on how to locate his hotel, which added a small measure of comfort to his growing anxiety.

As the bus lurched to a sudden stop, the occupants groaned, signalling that they would likely be stuck for a while. The irate clamour of frustrated Parisians surrounding him echoed his own rising tension. Doubt crept into his mind—had he made a mistake by booking this tour? Yet, the burning desire to uncover the mysteries of Uncle Henry's life quickly quelled any lingering apprehension. Amidst his restless thoughts, he felt the reassuring comfort of Frankie. The very presence brought him a sense of reassurance. He remembered the earlier chaos at customs, where questions had been hurled at him in rapid-fire French regarding Frankie's undeclared presence. That moment had been tense—the fear that their trip might be disrupted loomed large—but after a thorough security scan and a hurried, mostly inarticulate agreement, both he and Frankie had finally been granted entry into La Belle France. With each passing moment, the excitement of what lay ahead began to overshadow the hurdles of the journey.

CHAPTER FIVE

The bustling crowds ebbed and flowed along the Strand, their animated chatter woven with the distant sound of traffic. Some exuberant souls spilled into iconic Trafalgar Square, while others, laden with briefcases and wearied expressions, slithered down Villiers Street to the Embankment Tube, where computer drudges and salaried workers sought carriages to transport them to South-Eastern villages deemed to be suitable for daily commuters. Midst this confusion a few more tranquil souls ascended above the riotous noise to seek comfort and salutations within the Victorian walls of what was once, in 1865, the Charing Cross Railway Hotel, now a fashionable temporary residence for the incorrigible traveller.

In Suite 304, Mr. Henry Ritornel and Mrs. Alice Ritornel sat together, engrossed in a glossy travel brochure that promised a world of intrigue.

A MOTOR FLIGHT.

"And don't forget," Alice said with some acerbity, "if anyone on the tour asks, just tell them it's my birthday present to you." She rose from her seat, her podgy fingers fidgeting with the intricate lace collar of her dress as she walked toward the tea-making station. There, she switched off the kettle, which whistled cheerily as it reached a rolling boil. Henry watched her from the corner of his eye, bemused by the sway of her hips, which seemed more reminiscent of a drunken sailor than the glamorous screen siren Alice fancied herself to be emulating. Dressed in a bold floral print that stretched snugly around her curves, she had transformed over the years from the elegant young woman he had first known into what he now thought of as a lively Pillsbury Doughboy.

As Alice took a moment to glance at Henry's reflection in the mirror, a deep sigh escaped her lips. She brushed back strands of her bleached white hair that had fallen into her eyes, and with a newfound clarity, she saw him for who he truly was, a tall, lanky figure teetering on the brink of old age, with thinning hair that barely concealed his scalp, thin wrists poking from a thin shirt, and thin lips that had never been plump or persuasive.

"Birthday? Who's likely to ask?" Henry queried, breaking the silence.

Alice shrugged nonchalantly. "It could be anyone—just inquisitive minds wondering what brought us to this specific tour. We'd rather keep our plans under wraps; we don't want any hint of our project leaking out before we're fully prepared to make our pitch. Think of the millions we could earn."

Henry nodded, a flicker of interest crossing his face. "How many are booked?"

Alice placed the tea tray, adorned with two delicate cups and a small plate of biscuits, onto the table. "No more than eight," she replied. "I've told you—it's one of those exclusive tours for people who are genuinely intrigued by the subject matter."

Henry reached for a biscuit, his fingers brushing against the ornate plate sending one wafer to the floor. "And what about that guide woman?"

"Jenny? Jenny Forrest?" Alice said, pouring steaming tea into the cups.

"Yes, does she know what she's doing?"

Alice nodded, confidence lighting up her features. "She came highly recommended as the perfect person for the job, so I think we can trust her."

Henry gave a doubtful grunt, taking a sip of his tea while his mind wandered. Meanwhile, Alice, cup in hand, waddled toward the window, her eyes drawn to the outside world. The distant screech of car brakes pierced the air, momentarily distracting her, and she couldn't suppress a grin at the sight of a large woman sprawled comically across the bonnet of a taxi, her arms flung wide as if calling for the universe to take notice of her misadventure.

Henry muttered sourly into his tea, "More millions? How many more do we need?"

Alice turned to him. He's losing it, she thought to herself. His drive has gone. She said sharply "As we leave at seven in the morning at the station below, I suggest we have an early night."

CHAPTER SIX

In a nearby suite, Hazel Whitby leaned against the window frame, her brow furrowed with intrigue as she gazed down at the bustling streets below. "Why would anyone drag a corpse all the way from Nottingham to London?" she mused, her voice filled with both curiosity and disbelief. Londoners, oblivious to her musings, hurried away, seemingly ignoring the impressive replica of the Queen Eleanor Memorial Cross that stood proudly nearby. "I mean, how far is that?"

"A couple of hours by train, I suppose," replied Belinda Lawrence, her fingers deftly tying name tags to two small, stylish suitcases. "And who did the dragging?"

"Longshanks was his nickname. Tall fella. King Edward, and his wife was Eleanor of Castile. She fell off the twig up there and Eddie lugged her body back to bury her in Westminster Abbey."

"Sounds rather romantic," Belinda chimed in, flicking her gaze briefly to Hazel.

"Maybe," Hazel replied with a hint of uncertainty edging her tone. "I suspect he was just flexing his royal muscles." As she spoke, her attention was drawn away to a small, agitated group forming in the street below surrounding a policeman and a querulous couple. The screaming match between a taxi driver and a potential lawsuit was played out according to the rules.

"Also, was Eleanor stuffed or preserved in some way? I can't imagine she didn't start to be a bit whiffy by the time they arrived here. A touch of necromania, perhaps?"

Belinda remained silent, her focus on her phone as she scrutinized bank statements, making sure her cash card had enough funds for their upcoming adventures. A wave of nostalgia washed over her as she remembered the days of Travelers' Cheques and the unpredictability of exchange rates.

Not expecting an answer, Hazel further conjectured if Edward would think highly of the solitary tourist who paused just long enough to capture a blurry image of the Cross on his cell phone which, some weeks later back in Poughkeepsie, would be deleted in favour of an image from that night at the Ye Olde Cheshire Cheese and the blonde Swedish student who gave such good...

With a sigh, Hazel turned from the window, leaving the crowds behind, and re-entered the suite. She opened the tourist brochure she had been clutching tightly in her hands.

A MOTOR FLIGHT

"Do you think this is the room where they did it?" Hazel asked with a playful gleam in her eye.

"'It'?" Belinda responded, arching an eyebrow, intrigued.

"Yes. You know. 'IT,'" Hazel said, her tone teasing.

Belinda, amused, glanced up from the suitcase she was rummaging through. "Edith Wharton and Morton Fullerton? It's hard to say. It definitely was somewhere in this hotel where they had their, shall we say first encounter? Room ninety-one, wherever that is or was. But that was over a hundred years ago, and this hotel has been through quite the transformation with renovations and decor updates."

"What time do we leave in the morning?" Hazel asked.

Belinda, withdrawing a delicate nightgown from her suitcase, replied, "Seven-thirty down below at Charing Cross, so we'll need to leave here by seven."

Hazel tossed the brochure aside; her eager eyes roamed over the Room Service Menu. She impatiently scanned the list of enticing cocktails. "Must we take the ferry to Paris? Why not the fast train? Or even fly?"

"Because the tour commences in a certain way," Belinda explained patiently, not for the first time. "We're supposed to recreate the original motor trip that Edith and Henry James took, using the transport available during that time, or as close as possible."

"I still think we could do the tour ourselves without joining any organized group. We just have to follow the book about the motor flight," Hazel argued, a spark of defiance in her voice.

"That's true," Belinda admitted, "but think of

how much more enjoyable it will be. We won't have to fumble with booking hotels and hunting down restaurants. Plus, we could use a little pampering." Belinda's thoughts drifted back to the whirlwind summer they had experienced, bustling with tourists exploring their quaint antique shops— one nestled on Pulteney Bridge in Bath and the other in the charming town of Wells, Somerset. Her cottage, opened to coach tours, had drawn garden enthusiasts eager to pay homage to the celebrated landscape creator. This year, it had taken on a new twist, attracting ghouls who flocked to see the site that had once held the temporary grave of a murder victim. "Also," Belinda continued cautiously, "I don't think it would be wise for you to do all that driving. You know, driving on the right side like they do in France... When you're behind the wheel, you can be a bit... adventurous? Some might even call it... careless?"

But Hazel, absorbed in her own thoughts, brushed off the potential criticism of her driving skills. She was already on the phone with Room Service, ordering two Corpse Reviver cocktails. Her excitement was palpable as she envisioned the intoxicating blend of gin, Lillet Blanc, lime, orange liqueur, and a dash of absinthe awaiting her—a perfect beginning to their grand adventure.

CHAPTER SEVEN

As the sun began to rise, few travellers were boarding the train at Charing Cross, the station bustling with the early morning energy of a new day. Most wealthier passengers chose the speed of modern travel, zipping away like bats out of hell by fast train or plane, while those now taking their seats were a different breed: groups of wide-eyed students, elderly patrons reproducing romantic journeys from years past. A few humble, time affluent businessmen on poverty-stricken budgets completed the gathering.

Hazel settled into her aisle seat with a sigh, surrendering the coveted window seat to her friend Belinda, who leaned eagerly toward the glass. An Australian by birth, Belinda revelled in the sight of the English countryside gliding past, a patchwork of grassy fields and vibrant hedgerows. As they were to journey through Kent, she kept her mobile phone ready, to snap joyful pictures of any scene that captivated her eye.

Opening her book, **A Motor Flight Through France** by Edith Wharton, Hazel barely had time to immerse herself in the words when a robust woman barrelled down the aisle, her wide frame and oversized handbag creating a formidable barrier. With an ungracious, muttered "sorry," the woman pressed on, a whirlwind of movement that disrupted the serene atmosphere. Hazel stifled a sharp vulgarity, observing the woman was followed by a lanky man whose presence seemed equally disruptive. After a flurry of agitation and raised voices between the two, they finally took their seats, allowing the carriage to regain some semblance of former tranquillity.

Relieved that the raucous pair had settled away from her, and further cementing her belief that the wrong people travelled while the right people stayed at home, Hazel tried to dive back into her book. If she was going to spend the next week wandering through Edith Wharton's literary exploits while accompanied by Henry James, she might as well see what adventure, driven by Belinda's enthusiasm, she had agreed to pursue. It felt absurd to be on this tourist excursion at her age—fifty-five was supposed to be the new thirty-five, she reminded herself, though the twinge of pain in her hip suggested otherwise. As the train departed, the rhythmic sway of the carriage and the gentle hum of the tracks soon lulled her into a welcomed doze. She was woken by Belinda's gentle shake. "Wake up. We're at Dover Priory."

The ensuing hours did little to lighten Hazel's mood. At least the crossing of the Channel by ferry provided one small delight: the bar. Seated on a stool beneath a whimsical motto, "Live Life With No Excuses, Travel With No Regrets," she couldn't help but roll her eyes at the irony. As she sipped her first aperitif of the day, a glass of gin that usually calmed her frayed nerves, she found herself filled with a myriad of excuses and already regretting the venture. It wasn't the adventure itself that troubled her, but a gnawing sense of unease she couldn't quite name—a shadow of disquiet that hung over her.

Meanwhile, Belinda remained on deck, infatuated by the sight of the White Cliffs of Dover receding in the distance. The memories of her first glimpse of those majestic cliffs, twelve years prior as an eighteen-year-old backpacker arriving from Melbourne, flooded back to her. The thrill of new friendships and countless amateur sleuthing adventures with Hazel had brought them both to this point. Now, with their carefree tour through France on the horizon, she anticipated a refreshing escape from the weight of mystery and intrigue. But her reverie was abruptly interrupted by a loud voice barking commands. Turning, she spotted the hearty woman from the train with her tall, thin companion, theatrically posing for a steward. The poor man was on a mission to capture the perfect photo of them against the dramatic backdrop of the cliffs. Belinda smiled to herself, thankful that the boisterous woman was merely a fleeting distraction.

Finally, as the train from Calais pulled into Gare de Nord, the city's vibrant energy washed over them after a gruelling ten-hour journey from London. As they navigated the throngs of travellers in search of a taxi, a weary and disillusioned Hazel grumbled, "What new torture do you have in mind?"

Flipping open a glossy tour booklet, Belinda replied with enthusiasm, "Now we head to our hotel for the night. Our guide, Jenny Forrest, will be waiting for us, and tomorrow after breakfast, we'll embark on our tour."

Hazel, determined to maintain her foul mood, groaned in response. "I bet it's some grotty left bank dump complete with hard beds, cockroaches, and a primitive bidet."

Belinda glanced at the booklet. "I don't think so. It's the Duc de Crillon suite at Hotel de Crillon."

Hazel blinked in surprise, taking a deep breath and straightening her weary posture. For the first time, she mentally prepared her makeup and steeled herself for her entrance to an establishment that even she deemed worthy of her patronage. The promise of a luxurious stay began to soften the edges of her grumpiness, hinting at unexpected joys that lay ahead.

CHAPTER EIGHT

Hazel luxuriated in the opulence of the Hotel de Crillon, its grand chandeliers and exquisite decor reigniting her wanderlust. She almost suggested to Belinda that they abandon the tour and indulge in a prolonged stay within the hotel's elegant confines. The practicalities of cost momentarily slipped her mind; however, Belinda's scornful dismissal quickly jerked her back to reality, prompting Hazel to reluctantly get dressed as they prepared for the evening's meet-and-greet with the tour guide and fellow travellers, on the Terrace Marie-Antoinette, which offered a stunning view of the Place de la Concorde.

As they strolled through the hallway adorned with gilded mouldings and antique furnishings, Belinda remembered an article from the hotel's brochure. She reflected on the irony of the young Marie Antoinette taking piano lessons within these very walls, the former home of the Count of Crillon. Little did she know that just a few years later, she would be facing a raucous mob outside in the Place de la Révolution, ultimately meeting her fate at the hands of Madame la Guillotine.

A door further down the hallway opened, and Mr. Henry Ritornel emerged, his slender frame moving purposefully to the next room. He tapped lightly on the door, and Mrs. Alice Ritornel appeared in response. The couple exchanged a few sharp, hurried words, their voices barely above a whisper, before making their way toward the elevator. Belinda couldn't help but be disappointed that the noisy duo seemed destined to join the tour.

On the balcony, Jenny Forrest, the tour guide, surveyed the small group forming before her, her keen eyes scanning for potential challenges. Among them were the Ritornels, whom she remembered all too well from the moment they had overwhelmed her on arrival with an unending stream of questions about the upcoming itinerary. Despite her best efforts to free herself from their persistent inquiries, it had taken Mr. Henry's dramatic yawn to finally grant her a reprieve. Now, with the date she had arranged with the German woman, Astrid, slipping away, an annoyance simmered within her. She imagined Astrid waiting in vain at the bar on the Île St-Louis, only to realize she had essentially been stood up, leaving Jenny's mood decidedly less than cheerful.

A waiter appeared, elegantly presenting glasses of champagne—Krug Grande Cuvée—over which the group fell upon with the enthusiasm of Vikings plundering a treasure trove. As they raised their glasses, a glimmer of anticipation danced in the air. Jenny glanced down at the dossier, a neatly organized collection of details about each person on the tour, before looking back at the assembled group of travellers.

One particular figure stood out among them—a portly man in a linen suit that had likely once graced his frame beautifully. Now, the fabric strained against his girth, and the buttons threatened to pop free, betraying the extent to which he had savoured the carte du jour offerings. This had to be Obadiah James. His walk was slightly mincing, and thin wireframe spectacles perched precariously on his nose, reminiscent of a pince-nez. With a breathless and eager voice that bubbled over with enthusiasm, combined with thinning silver hair, he struck Jenny as an oversized child, awkwardly navigating his first unsupervised outing. A smirk tugged at her lips as she observed Obadiah struggling to engage the unyielding ZeZe Dupont in conversation, his efforts being met with little success.

CHAPTER NINE

ZeZe, a well-known activist and fierce advocate for preserving the nuances of French history and culture, stood in sharp contrast to the chaos around her. To Jenny, she seemed cool and aloof, her slight frame and languorous auburn hair masking a steely resolve. ZeZe was much smaller than her daunting stature on television, where she was a formidable force, relentlessly confronting anyone who dared oppose her views. Yet beneath her delicate exterior lay the heart of a skilled fighter; she had navigated countless battles in her decades-long career as a media heavyweight. Jenny mused for a moment on ZeZe's choice to create this tour through quaint French villages. It struck her that people would think it somewhat peculiar, given the depth of her historical knowledge. It had all the hallmarks of a busman's holiday—but perhaps there was more to it than met the eye...

Walton Anderson and Joan Smith, both in their twenties—one hailing from the sun-drenched landscapes of Nevada and the other from the bustling streets of Chicago—were about to continue on an exciting adventure through Europe. Their enthusiasm for the journey was as relevant as their disinterest in the Theory of Relativity; it had little bearing on their everyday lives. However, with most of their friends already having ticked off European tours from their bucket lists, they were determined not to be left behind. Joan erupted into a high-pitched, contagious laugh that echoed across the gathering. Jenny sighed softly, her instincts warning her that complaints and discontent might soon follow.

Her attention was then drawn to two other newcomers: Hazel and Belinda, two single women entering the scene. Their arrival brought a fresh energy, and Jenny swiftly checked their names off her list before tapping her pen against a delicate champagne glass to gather the group's attention.

"Ladies and gentlemen, good evening, and welcome to our motor tour!" she announced, her voice vibrant with command. "As you already know, we will be retracing the route taken by the illustrious writers Edith Wharton and Henry James as they journeyed through the captivating landscapes of France back in 1907. Although we won't be traversing the countryside in Edith's newly invented motorcar, a Panhard-Levassor, I assure you that the charabanc we've selected is as vintage as we could find while still ensuring your comfort. Edith claimed her luxurious Panhard-Levassor had been bought with the proceeds of her last novel. Henry James replied, from proceeds of his last novel he purchased a hand barrow. With the proceeds from his next novel he would have it painted."

Walton and Joan exchanged puzzled glances, their curiosity piqued. "Er...what exactly is a sharahbang?" Walton inquired, his brow furrowed.

With a tight smile, Jenny elaborated, "The charabanc was an early form of a bus, a popular choice for 'works outings' that businesses once organized for their employees. However, critics often argued it served less as a mode of transport and more as a vehicle for revellers and raucous troublemakers." Joan instinctively grasped Walton's hand, alarmed at the potential mischief that awaited them. "Most charabanc excursions, however," Jenny continued with a hint of tartness, "were surprisingly tame, and I expect ours to follow suit." She delivered this with a well-practiced, stiff smile, signalling her intent to maintain decorum throughout the trip. To shield herself from the group's blank stares, she immersed herself in the detailed itinerary. "There is one more companion who is running a bit late but should be joining us shortly," she continued, scanning the crowd. "As for Gino, our driver, he is in charge of managing your luggage. He is mute but possesses impressive hearing, so if you have questions, don't anticipate a verbal response. The charabanc accommodates twenty-six passengers, providing ample room for your belongings."

As anticipation filled the air, Jenny shifted gears. "Tonight, we have a delightful surprise: dinner at a marvellous restaurant nearby that specializes in traditional Normandy cooking. I invite you to follow me as we delve into the culinary secrets once explored by Edith Wharton and Henry James." Her words carried a promise of adventure and discovery, hinting at the rich history and delectable fare awaiting them.

CHAPTER TEN

The Parisian morning light revealed the vibrant yellow 1929 Burlingham-bodied Leyland Lioness charabanc. The vehicle stood patiently, its hood thrown back to expose plush leather seats that seemed to beckon travellers into an adventure. Nearby, the driver, Gino Marcato, was a slight figure with dark hair and wiry limbs, invoking the image of a bantam-weight boxer ready for a match.

"Another new hell," groaned Hazel, her voice laced with mockery. "What have you got me into this time?"

"Be quiet and just get on board," Belinda insisted, gently propelling her reluctant friend toward the charabanc's door. With a huff of resignation, Hazel slid into the seat behind the driver, casting a judgmental gaze at their fellow travellers as they filed in. Belinda followed and whispered, "Take a look at our hostess." They observed Jenny as she stepped away from the charabanc, her demeanour brisk as she glanced at her watch and pulled out her phone. Frustration crossed her face as she punched in a number and received no response, prompting her to return to the vehicle with a frown. "Let's get going. Our first stop is the Père-Lachaise Cemetery."

The sight of the open charabanc traversing Paris's magical streets drew the curiosities of tourists, who marvelled at the spectacle and speculated on the odd assortment of passengers. Mobile phones recorded the scene for future laughs; on day five of their Ten Day, Ten Town Tour marketed to uninspired thrill-seeking retirees, they assumed the mobile travellers to be local eccentrics, perfect fodder for stories to share around dinner tables back home. Indigenous Parisians, having seen everything there is to see, turned a blind eye.

The mid-morning calm atmosphere of the famed cemetery, denied the confusion of famous souls resting beneath the weight of massive stones, trapping them forever in a tangible world. Wandering past these memorials the group was hushed and any initial excitement anticipated by the journey soon dissipated into a respectful tribute.

Leading her group like a mother duck guiding her ducklings, Jenny began her narrative. "Père Lachaise takes its name from Père François de la Chaise, the confessor to King Louis XIV, the Sun King. He once lived in a religious house on this very site."

ZeZe lingered behind with Gino, a fact not lost on Belinda, who seized the moment to observe the dynamics of her new companions. It appeared as if ZeZe scrutinized each person, her discerning eyes assessing their worth. Belinda's gaze shifted to Mr. Henry and Mrs. Alice, who were deep in a conspiratorial whispering, seemingly unaware of the illustrious tombs around them. Obadiah was busy capturing images of every tomb as he passed, a digital record for proof of his visit to this famed necropolis, should anyone back home in North Carolina doubt his adventure—though Belinda doubted anyone would even care. Walton and Joan, seemingly unimpressed by the surroundings, only perked up when they stumbled upon the tomb of Jim Morrison, which seemed cramped between two more grandiose graves. Here was someone they could relate to. A modest array of flowers adorned the site, accompanied by faded photographs of the pop star in his prime, alongside liquor bottles, remnants of substances, and an assortment of trinkets, each carrying a story, that were undoubtedly tributes filled with bittersweet nostalgia for mourners honouring their youth rather than the artistry of a long-gone talent.

"Remember that wherever your heart is, there you will find your treasure," Jenny's voice, sharp and commanding, broke the silence as the group halted before a tomb. "We are at Chopin's final resting place." She continued, "While this diversion is not strictly part of the original Motor Flight that Edith and Henry embarked upon, we will be spending time later at George Sand's Maison in Nohant, where much can be said about Chopin, as he and Sand shared a profound love."

Drawing closer, the group admired the exquisite marble statue *La Musique en pleurs*, gracefully poised atop the rectangular stone tomb. "The statue represents Euterpe, the muse of music,"

Jenny explained, her voice filled with admiration. "The front showcases a medallion depicting Chopin in profile, based on a cast taken shortly after his death. This monument was inaugurated on the first anniversary of Chopin's passing..."

Jenny's words trailed off as she noticed something in the distance, prompting her to step away from the tomb. All heads turned to see what had captivated her attention, a tall, sharply dressed man making his way toward them. As he approached Jenny, they engaged in a low-spoken conversation that seemed tinged with tension, yet an underlying familiarity sparked a momentary connection. When the moment passed, they returned to join the rest of the group. ZeZe, distracted from her phone, regarded the newcomer with a sceptical eye, a hint of judgment etched on her features.

"I'd like to introduce our final guest," Jenny announced. "Mr. Andre Levinz." Andre offered a tight smile, shrugging slightly. "You'll forgive my tardiness... airlines, you know. The Wright Brothers' schedule."

Belinda noticed Gino was studying the newcomer with an intensity that intrigued her. As everyone reboarded the charabanc, Andre settled into a seat at the rear. Belinda turned to Hazel, only to find her eyes trailing after him, a glint of interest illuminating her gaze. Belinda recognized that look from years gone by, realizing that over the course of the tour, she would witness Hazel prowling like a cat in search of a mate.

"Now, finally," Jenny said, her tone firm yet filled with anticipation, "we are on our motor flight."

CHAPTER ELEVEN

Strolling along the centuries-old, cobbled streets of Amiens, Belinda and Hazel moved with their group, taking in the colourful atmosphere of the city. The air was tinged with the tantalizing aromas of local cuisines, setting the stage for an unforgettable evening. Hazel, after some internal debate, had come to terms with her situation and clung to the hope of sharing meaningful moments with Andre. Meanwhile, Belinda was captivated by the grandeur of France's largest Gothic cathedral, its intricate details and soaring spires leaving her in awe. Yet, fatigue weighed heavily on them both after a long day of exploration, and the prospect of a hearty meal followed by a cozy bed was immensely appealing.

After savouring the last bite of her delicious Tarte Tatin, Belinda let out a contented sigh, reclining back in her chair with a sense of satisfaction. Around her at small tables, the other diners appeared lost in their own worlds, each absorbed in their own experiences. Near the window, the American couple seemed an odd fit for the occasion. They sat scrutinizing their plates, sceptical of the Clafoutis before them, with Joan's sharp voice lamenting the absence of her favorite Pierogi, a dish she longed for. Across the room, the elderly couple was wholly immersed in their meal, indulging in their apple, gin, and juniper tarte tatin with enthusiasm. Mrs. Alice muttered simple phrases in her practiced, if faltering, French, and

Mr. Henry, with a blank expression, responded with occasional disinterested nods.

In stark contrast, Obadiah sat alone at his table, a cloud of grim expressions marring his features. He meticulously removed his glasses, polishing them intently with his napkin as if the clarity of his vision could dispel his discomfort. Once they were cleaned, he returned his glasses to his face, staring blankly at the remnants of his meal as if pondering life's great questions.

Across the room, ZeZe and Andre occupied separate tables. ZeZe finishing her Mousse au Chocolat, with a flick of elegance and a number of diamond rings flashing on her fingers, lifted her napkin to daintily wipe her mouth before savouring another sip of wine, her demeanour poised and composed Andre, however, seemed absorbed in his mobile phone, his expression distant and engrossed.

Belinda feigned a cough, just enough to draw Hazel's attention. "Don't you think this is a curious mix of people for a tour like this?" she mused, a hint of intrigue lacing her words.

Before Hazel could respond, a sudden movement caught their attention. Obadiah abruptly stood and strode purposefully toward Andre's table. He leaned in closely, whispering something that sent a flicker of surprise across Andre's face. Shaking his head emphatically, Andre made it clear that he was dismissing whatever Obadiah had suggested. With the weight of rejection hanging in the air, Obadiah stepped back, turned on his heel, and exited the room in a hurry. A heavy silence enveloped the dining area as each person exchanged perplexed glances with their companions, curiosity etched on their faces. ZeZe, unable to hide her amusement, stifled a smile behind her napkin.

Andre looked around at the bewildered group and shrugged, a mixture of confusion and weariness in his gaze. "It has definitely been a long day," he remarked, "I suppose the young man is simply overexcited." Yet for Belinda and Hazel, this unexpected moment marked the intriguing start of a mystery.

CHAPTER TWELVE

"What do you think that was all about?" Hazel inquired, her voice laced with curiosity as she ducked her head to avoid the sloping, weathered beams of the ancient bedroom. This historic building, now transformed into a hotel, retained all the quirks and inconveniences that came with its long history. Belinda maneuverer herself awkwardly between her bed and the wall, a slight frown on her face. "Who knows? Obadiah is American, Andre is... French? German? What could they possibly have in common?"

With a soft sigh of contentment, Hazel slid beneath her covers, pleasantly surprised by the unexpected comfort of the mattress. "That's for them to know and for us to find out. It's after midnight, though. Let's turn off the light and get some sleep."

"Oh, wait!" Belinda exclaimed suddenly. "I left my toothbrush in the bathroom." Without another moment's hesitation, she whisked herself out into the dim hallway and made her way to the restroom. After rummaging through the small space, she located her toothbrush and turned to leave but froze as she noticed a door further down the corridor creaking open.

Mr. Henry stepped out, his expression tense as he exchanged a few sharp words with Mrs. Alice, who stood nearby. He then made his way to the next room, entering it with a swift motion, the slamming of both doors echoing ominously in the silent hallway.

Just as the air settled, another door opened, and Obadiah appeared. He was dressed casually in a loose shirt and worn jeans, his expression thoughtful as he shut the door behind him with a gentle click. Almost like a phantom in the night, he tiptoed down the staircase, disappearing into the shadows cast by the flickering hallway lights.

Belinda, momentarily feeling as though she were privy to a scene from a Georges Feydeau Farce, let her curiosity ignite. She hurried back to her room, bursting through the door with excitement. "You'll never guess what I just saw!" she whispered animatedly, but the only response was the steady rhythm of Hazel's soft breathing; she had already slipped into the deep embrace of sleep.

The next morning, breakfast was served in the sun-drenched garden, the air filled with the enticing aroma of freshly baked croissants and rich coffee. The travellers savoured these culinary delights, their senses awakening to the day ahead. Jenny, the ever-energetic guide, called their attention. "We leave in ten minutes for Beauvais, so if everyone could kindly gather at the charabanc, we will begin our journey." She diligently counted heads, her brow furrowing slightly. "It seems Obadiah must be sleeping in. Gino, dear, please go and fetch him, and don't forget his suitcase."

Before Gino could rise from his seat, Belinda stood abruptly, her eyes glinting with determination. "I'll go get him. I need to grab my handbag anyway." She dashed up the stairs, the worn carpet muffling her hurried footsteps. Upon reaching Obadiah's door, she knocked softly but received no answer. Curiosity tinged with worry prompted her to gently twist the doorknob and push the door open. The room was deserted. Sunlight streamed through the window, illuminating the neat bed, untouched by sleep. All that remained of Obadiah was an open suitcase overflowing with neatly folded clothes. Amidst his belongings, she spotted a sleek black object with an antenna, which she surmised was an old-fashioned mobile phone. A collection of documents rested on top, inviting her to investigate further. As she sifted through the papers, Belinda discovered they primarily focused on Henry James, showcasing photographs and articles that hinted at a deeper narrative. Among them, one file stood out, labelled in bold letters: MORTON FULLERTON. Questions hung in the air, setting the stage for the unfolding story.

CHAPTER THIRTEEN

The departure to Beauvais lingered in the air, temporarily suspended as hotel staff and groundskeepers conducted a thorough search. Frustration creased Jenny's brow; the delay was intolerable. With a sigh, she picked up her phone, contacting the local police to report a missing passenger. The prevailing assumption was he had simply wandered off, lost in the winding paths of the quaint French village. However, the tour couldn't pause indefinitely for one wayward traveller; Obadiah's suitcase had been stowed among the others, and should he turn up, he would need to find his own way to the next scheduled stop.

As the charabanc continued its journey through the lush countryside, where ripe foods were being gathered: corn, maize, alongside pumpkins, apples, and golden fields of harvested wheat. Hazel tied a scarf over her hair; the wind whipped around her, teasing strands into wild disarray.

"I saw Obadiah leave his room and go down the stairs last night," Belinda confided softly, her voice barely rising above the hum of the engine to prevent the others from overhearing.

"Did you mention that to anyone?" Hazel asked, curious.

"I told Jenny, but she brushed it off. She didn't seem to care at all that he was missing; her main concern was keeping the tour on schedule," Belinda replied, frowning slightly.

Hazel's brow furrowed. "I'd like to know what he discussed with Andre. The first chance I get, I'll ask him."

"Something else I found odd," Belinda continued, her voice lowered conspiratorially, "was I saw Mr. Henry leave Mrs. Alice and go to a different bedroom."

"Maybe hers had a single bed," Hazel suggested.

"No, all the rooms are doubles," Belinda countered, shaking her head.

"Perhaps she snores?" Hazel ventured.

"That could be, but I thought it strange for a married couple to sleep apart. I'm pretty sure they had an argument."

The group's stop in Beauvais was brief due to their late arrival, limiting their sightseeing to the picturesque Place de l'Hôtel de Ville and the enchanting old streets bordering the grand cathedral. Hazel, drawn by the charm of houses dating back to the 12th to 16th centuries, strolled leisurely, savouring the feeling of history beneath her feet. Turning a corner, her heart quickened when she spotted Andre seated at a small café, the sunlight catching the gleam of his hair. Taking this as fate's whimsical nudge, she adjusted her stride, hoping to exude an alluring confidence as she approached him.

"Excuse me," she said, her voice both warm and inviting. "We really haven't had a proper chance to get acquainted."

Andre stood, his demeanour courteous as he gestured for her to join him. Hazel sank into the chair opposite, a glow of pleasure lighting her features. "I'm Hazel, and I've been eager to say hello."

"And I've been eager to meet you," Andre replied, his smile genuine. "What brings you on a tour like this?"

Hazel hesitated, contemplating honesty. Should she admit that she'd rather be nestled back at the hotel in Paris than shuttling through rural France alongside her travel companion? However, the thought that Andre might be passionate about antiquities and ancient towns prompted her to alter her response. "Oh, I'm devoted to history, and I've read works by Henry James and Edith Wharton."

"Ah yes," Andre said, his eyes lighting up with recognition. "James. Do you have a favorite work of his?"

A sudden panic gnawed at Hazel. Surely she could recall one of James's books. Flashes of film adaptations crossed her mind, fragments of a story about a governess and eerie children... what was it called?

Matchmaker?

No.

The Secret Garden?

No.

Her memory seemed to fail her, and she softly muttered in frustration, "Screw it!"

"Ah, yes, The Turn of the Screw," Andre interjected, catching the whispered fragment. "A masterpiece. James was quite the character. He was very close with Edith Wharton, yet there are whispers he was also drawn to her lover, Morton Fullerton, though it's all hearsay."

Grateful for Andre's ability to redirect the conversation, Hazel seized the opportunity to shift subjects, aware that he might ask for more titles. "I'm fascinated by your accent. I can't quite place it. Is it German?"

Andre flinched ever so slightly. "No, you are mistaken. I am Polish." With a gesture to the waiter, he continued, "And now, to celebrate our newfound friendship, let's share a glass of wine."

Hazel shifted in her seat, allowing her coat to slide from her shoulders. Andre noticed this discreetly from the corner of his eye and smiled inwardly. He selected a bottle from the menu, settling back comfortably as he admired her presence: a mature woman, still captivating, radiating an air of possibility.

"What do you make of our companions?" Hazel inquired, glancing around the café, "It's a curious group, mostly Americans. And that Obadiah. He's certainly the oddest among us. What did he whisper to you at dinner? We've all been dying to know."

Andre chuckled softly. "Nothing worth dying over, I assure you. He asked me about a companion of Henry James and if I knew anything about him."

"Oh? Who was that?"

As the waiter poured their selected wine, Andre nodded acceptance. "Who? Oh, Morton Fullerton."

CHAPTER FOURTEEN

Belinda stepped out of the imposing Cathedral of Saint-Pierre, a magnificent but unfinished structure that soared above her. The intricate stonework and towering spires caught the fading light of the late afternoon sun, casting shadows across the cobblestone square. As she flipped through her guidebook, she marvelled at the tales of relentless structural disasters that had plagued the cathedral over the centuries, from financial hardships and the devastation of the Great Plague of 1348 to the turmoil of the Hundred Years' War. Though only the grand choir remained intact as the main church building, Belinda found herself utterly enchanted by the history and artistry that surrounded her.

Nearby, she noticed Mr. Henry and Mrs. Alice, also captivated by the cathedral's façade. Mr. Henry had set up a semi-professional video camera on a tripod, while Mrs. Alice scribbled notes in a weathered notebook. At first glance, they seemed like the quintessential extreme tourists, destined to bore their friends with endless footage of their journey. Yet, a deeper look at their focused expressions hinted at a genuine appreciation for the art and culture. They had maintained a deliberate distance from the other members of the tour, retreating into the solitude of their hotel rooms immediately after dinner. Belinda considered their age might be a factor, the toll of travel and physical activity weighing heavily on them. However, her curiosity was piqued by the memory of watching an angry Mr. Henry slip away from Mrs. Alice's room long after midnight, casting an intriguing shadow over their sombre personas.

As Belinda ventured onto Rue Saint-Pierre, she paused in a small, tree-filled square that exuded an air of serenity. Across the street, she caught sight of ZeZe, who appeared to be passionately engaged in conversation with herself—or so it seemed. Her curiosity ignited, Belinda cautiously inched closer, excited by the thrill of eavesdropping. ZeZe was indeed speaking animatedly, but it was not to herself; a two-man film crew, replete with camera and sound equipment, was recording her every word.

Though Belinda's grasp of French was limited, she caught scattered fragments of ZeZe's rapid-fire speech: "Nohant," and, strikingly, "Disneyland, non, non, non!" The latter exclamation carried a vigorous shake of her head that conveyed her strong feelings. The interview lasted just a minute, and when it ended, ZeZe animatedly conversed with the crew as they gathered their equipment.

Belinda pressed herself against the cool stone of the cathedral, hoping to avoid detection. As the crew walked by, the cameraman, a lanky figure with an easy smile, caught her eye and flashed her a cheeky grin, before he continued on.

Nearby, Hazel and Andre made their way back to their hotel, invigorated by the wine they had enjoyed. The air was filled with the laughter of tourists and the distant sound of street musicians. "What is it about Henry James and Edith Wharton that intrigues you?" Hazel asked, her voice light as she playfully brushed against his arm.

"Honestly? Nothing much. I'm just eager to reach the next town, Nohant," Andre replied, his gaze drifting into the distance as if he could already envision their journey.

"Why is that?" Hazel queried, her lack of true curiosity evident in her tone. She had slipped into a reverie, envisioning a romantic stroll beside Andre down a chic street in Warsaw, the lilting melodies of Chopin's nocturnes drifting around them.

"Because Henry and Edith were captivated by George."

The name sparked a faint recognition in Hazel, and she rummaged through her memory for a connection. *Formby?*

"George and Frédéric Chopin were lovers," Andre elaborated, his voice taking on a more serious tone.

Hazel was jolted from her daydream. "Of course... George Sand. That was the pen name of that remarkable female author—what was her name? Aurore Dupin Dudevant, am I right? She was French..."

"And Chopin was Polish," Andre confirmed, passion igniting in his eyes. "They shared a love affair that spanned nine years, living together at George's house in Nohant, an enchanting place he dubbed the 'Black Valley.'"

"And what do you hope to discover in Nohant?" Hazel asked, genuinely curious now.

Andre turned to her, his expression serious and thoughtful. "I believe we will uncover something of great significance to Poland and its people. You could say it is the very heart of Poland."

CHAPTER FIFTEEN

As evening set in, Belinda and Hazel sat in their bedroom, engaged in a deep discussion about the day's strange events. Belinda recounted ZeZe's video interview, her brow furrowed in confusion. "What could possibly prompt her to mention Disneyland?"

"A Minnie Mouse fetish, perhaps?" Hazel suggested sarcastically. However, her tone quickly shifted as she recalled her earlier conversation with Andre. "What I do know is Andre is definitely up to something intriguing involving Poland."

Belinda leaned forward, genuinely interested. "Then why is he here, on tour in France? Did he reveal anything important?"

Hazel, now applying face cream filling the air with a floral scent, shook her head. "He didn't provide any specifics. He only said that it's related to Nohant and holds significant importance for the Poles. There was also something about hearts."

Belinda's curiosity intensified at the mention of Nohant. "Both of them mentioned Nohant. What's so compelling about that place?" She reached for the tour schedule, her fingers tracing the printed words. "Nohant... George Sand... and Chopin..."

"Exactly, Andre mentioned Chopin," Hazel confirmed, as she paused in attempting to moderate her facial wrinkles.

"And Chopin was undeniably Polish. What secrets does he think he'll uncover?" Belinda pressed on, her mind racing with possibilities.

With a decisive gesture, Hazel put down the face cream and reached for a glass of rich, amber liqueur, savouring its warmth as she took a sip. "Who knows? Let's forget it for the moment and see if there's anything worth watching on TV." The screen flickered to life, showcasing the familiar scenes of Parisian chaos, where students squared off against the police. Hazel let out a weary sigh, glancing at the TV guide before declaring, "Switch to streaming. CinemaTroll may have some films worth our time."

Belinda swiftly changed the channel, just as a lavish film about life at the opulent court of Louis XVI began to fade. The end credits rolled like a languid river, accompanied by the grand March of the Kings by Lully, which echoed through the room, enhancing the dramatic atmosphere.

Screenplay by Evelyn Cronk
Directed by Peter Lamb
Produced by Clifton Davidson
As the final title appeared, Belinda gasped.
Executive Producers
Alice Ritornel
Henry Ritornel.

CHAPTER SIXTEEN

IMDB personal biographies, plot summaries, trivia, ratings, and fan and critical reviews.

The text sprinted across the computer screen. "It's a website about films and you can read details about filmmakers," said Belinda. Hazel took a sip of her liqueur as Belinda typed in Mr Henry and Mrs Alice's names.

A list of films produced by them unfolded on the screen.

TUDOR TEMPTRESS: Henry VIII Secret Wife

JOAN OF ARC: Woman on Fire

REVOLUTIONARY ROMANCE: The Sapphic Secrets of Marie Antionette's love life

CALIGULA: Emperor of Lust

Hazel choked on her drink. "There wouldn't be a dry seat in the cinema!"

"I'll try their biographies," said Belinda. A few taps on the keys and the screen revealed an unexpected truth.

The Ritornels started their career with the short film 'Bend Over Backwards, Mary Jane', a study of College life. They made their first feature film 'Keep Cutting The Mustard', before going on to produce a string of big-budget dramas based on the lives of historical figures. The Ritornels famed as a husband-and-wife team are actually, brother and sister.

There was little sleep for Belinda and Hazel as they reviewed the strange happenings and the behaviour of their traveling companions. They dismissed the young American couple, as Joan had revealed, rather dejectedly, Walton would have preferred to go camping in Yellowstone National Park whereas she hankered after Niagara Falls in the hope the romantic setting would finally convince Walton to propose. As their holiday was coming to an end they'd joined the tour at the last moment, welcoming the idea they didn't have to deal with language problems and a brutal maître d'hôtel. But the remaining travellers were another story.

The revelation that the Ritornels were filmmakers and brother and sister was considered. "That explains the separate bedrooms and the camera I saw them using," said Belinda, "but their films were big-screen historical sagas costing millions. Why are they filming this tour?"

"Then the sudden disappearance of Obadiah and tour guide Jenny's apparent lack of concern," said Hazel.

"I've just remembered," said Belinda, "you recall when I was in Obadiah's room the day he went missing, I found a file marked, Morton Fullerton? He was Edith's lover, and they first did IT, made love in that hotel in London. We wondered which room they had been in, remember?"

Hazel nodded. "A bit of a comedown for Edith, a bonk in a grotty railway hotel, as it would have been then. I imagine she had planned for roses and champagne, bluebirds, and a string quartet. Instead, she probably got grubby sheets, pigeons, and the sounds of costermongers flogging sooty cabbage and potatoes down in the Strand. And there's another thing. Henry James was not averse to Morton's lure... or so it was noised."

Belinda raised a questioning eyebrow. "So why did Obadiah have a file on him?" she pondered.

"And then there's Andre. Mr Mysterious. A Pole intent on visiting Nohant and George Sand's house? OK, so Chopin got his leg over there...what's so special about that?"

Belinda shook her head. "They're a weird mob, that's for sure, and ZeZe with her camera team, appears to be making a documentary. But about what?" The early morning light brought an end to the speculation but sparked new questions as they prepared to depart for Nohant.

CHAPTER SEVENTEEN

"The Church of Saint-Anne dates back to the eleventh or twelfth century," Jenny said, her voice echoing softly in the dim interior. "I know it's somewhat challenging to see, but if you look closely, you can still appreciate some of the original wall paintings."

The waning autumn afternoon light struggled to penetrate the heavy gloom that enveloped the cracked stone walls of the small church. As Hazel took a step forward, her foot caught on a broken floor tile. She muttered a characteristically irreverent comment, but Jenny, undeterred by the blasphemy, continued her explanation, "These paintings, though faded by centuries, are still treasures worth valuing. Remember, we are just across from the house of George Sand here in Nohant, and tomorrow we will visit the Maison. Soon, we'll move to our accommodations in the nearby village of Saint-Chartier. Take your time viewing the paintings while I contact the hotel."

With that, she glided into the encroaching darkness, the soft rustle of her movements almost ghostly. Hazel fished her mobile phone from her pocket and flicked on the flashlight, its weak beam slicing through the dim interior. With renewed focus, she and Belinda cautiously navigated the confined space, the other members of their group fading like phantoms into the shadows. The lingering stillness, was punctuated only by the shuffle of feet on the ancient stone floor and the occasional hushed whisper of awe as the group examined the faint, peeling images that adorned the walls. Time passed imperceptibly, and as if sharing an unspoken understanding, the group gradually made their way to the door, stepping into the churchyard now shrouded in almost complete darkness. As they moved toward the waiting charabanc the sky stretched above them, a vast canopy of deep indigo.

Without warning, a shrill scream pierced the tranquil silence of the village.

Their hearts pounding, the group froze except for Belinda who instinctively moved toward the source of the cry. She collided with Mrs. Alice, who was now in a panic, still screaming in terror. Hazel quickly switched on her phone's flashlight again, the beam illuminating the ground before her.

There, lying portentously at her feet, was a single black leather glove...its ominous presence a chilling token of the unknown lurking in the shadows.

The pool of light widened to encompass the body of Mr Henry at the foot of a memorial cross.

His skull had been crushed by the severed head of a stone Angel.

CHAPTER EIGHTEEN

Hazel squirmed uncomfortably in her seat, the charabanc's frame creaking softly as it lumbered along the winding road. The vehicle's hood billowed over the passengers, offering an odd mix of protection and concealment as they ventured deeper into the afternoon haze on their way back to Nohant. In Belinda's mind, the roads were lively with townsfolk, their voices rising in unison, pointing accusatorily and shouting "J'accuse!" Imagining the scene made her pulse race.

Across the aisle, Ze Ze's face wore a mask of stoic indifference, while Andre sank into the small glow of his mobile phone, seeking solace in the digital world. Joan clung nervously to Walton, who was trying to embody Alpha Male energy. The tension in the air was palpable.

Hazel was trapped in a brown study of hunger. The group had spent a restless night and the following morning at the Commissariat de Police in Châteauroux, where they were interrogated under harsh fluorescent lights and made to provide statements concerning the shocking murder of Mr. Henry. The police had ordered them to remain in Nohant for the foreseeable future, a directive that gnawed at Hazel's patience. "Sixteen hours without so much as a cup of tea—just an invasive cheek swab for DNA," she huffed, her voice laced with annoyance.

"Well, they *are* investigating a murder,"

Belinda replied, her tone steady but soft.

"And now we're stuck in this awful place until God knows when!" Hazel exclaimed, her frustration boiling over.

"I wouldn't go so far as to call Nohant awful. We did plan to visit here, remember? So just take a deep breath. We can explore and maybe solve a murder. When we finally reach our hotel, you can relax with a nice cup of tea," Belinda reassured.

Hazel cast a disapproving glance out the window. "More like a gin and tonic. What kind of hotel are we even staying at?"

"It's an old convent or Priory in a nearby village, Saint-Chartier," Belinda explained, a hint of enthusiasm in her voice.

Hazel groaned, picturing a cold, stone cell with hard, unyielding furniture. "Just what I need—sleeping like a monk on a stone bed."

"I promise, even if it is a 12th-century Priory, it will have modern conveniences," Belinda assured her.

"Like flagellation." Hazel remained unconvinced.

The charabanc turned off the main road, veering toward the Priory. As the rolling landscape rushed by, vibrating with shades of yellow and green Belinda, attempting to quell the irritation emanating from Hazel, was drawn back to gaze at the scenery. Unexpectedly, she gasped, her eyes widening in disbelief as she clutched Hazel's arm. "Look!"

Hazel frowned as she followed Belinda's gaze. A familiar figure was making its way toward the main road—a rotund body clad in shirt and jeans, thin spectacles glinting in the afternoon light. It was Obadiah James.

As they arrived at the Priory, the chapel had been transformed into a charming restaurant, its high, arched ceilings and modest stone walls still whispering tales of sacred history. A few incomplete wall paintings lingered like ghosts of the past, veiling the space in a sense of solemnity.

The group settled down after their late lunch, relaxing in the peaceful ambiance, when Jenny stood up to address them, her tone grave. "As you're all aware, the police have requested that we remain in the area for the foreseeable future as they investigate the circumstances surrounding Mr. Henry's murder. I know this situation is shocking and distressing, but we must comply with the police's demands." Her eyes swept across the table, capturing the tension etched on each face. "They will no doubt have more questions for us until the case is resolved. This means another intrusion into our lives," she continued, explaining that the police would be inspecting the luggage and belongings of each group member. A low murmur of discontent rippled through the room, the weight of their new status as suspects hanging heavily in the air.

"What do they expect to find?" Andre asked, furrowing his brow.

Jenny shrugged lightly, her eyes darting as though contemplating possible evidence. "Well, firstly, the left-hand black glove that matches the one presumably used in the murder, I suppose. They might search for anything else they think is relevant to the crime."

"But surely the murderer would have disposed of anything incriminating," Hazel interjected, her voice tinged with concern. "When can we expect the police?"

"They're on their way," Jenny responded, trying to reassure them.

"And what about Mrs. Alice?" Belinda asked, her expression softening with worry.

"She is in shock and under police surveillance in the hospital. She'll remain there until they release Mr. Henry's body. Now I suggest you rest as best you can, because tomorrow we finally get to Nohant and La Maison de George Sand."

The group rose, some grumbling about the perceived further invasion of their privacy, as they were led to their rooms to recover from the emotional turmoil. Only Belinda and Hazel lingered, watching as the maid cleared away the remnants of the meal. Jenny paused at the door, casting a concerned glance back at them. She hesitated, as if pondering whether to say something, but ultimately turned away without a word.

Belinda took a slow sip of her coffee, her brow furrowed in thought. "So, Obadiah beat us to Nohant. How and why?"

"Perhaps he didn't want to be stuck in our company," Hazel replied, her focus shifting to the dinner menu as she tried to distract herself from the growing anxiety.

"And we never found out why he asked Andre about Morton Fullerton that first night," Belinda mused, her eyes distant.

Hazel resolved to order the 'Pavé de saumon à l'unilatéral et riz kikoman' for dinner, momentarily lost in thoughts of culinary delight. "I'm far more interested in finding out who killed Mr. Henry. And why?"

Belinda nodded in agreement. "We were all in the church—" "In the dark," Hazel interrupted, her tone sharp. "Remember I used my phone's torch to see those wall paintings? I can't imagine how anyone else could see in the dark. It's entirely possible that anyone could have slipped outside and attacked Mr. Henry."

"Yes," Belinda conceded, her voice low. "And Jenny vanished into the dark after she claimed she would call this hotel. Did she stay inside or slip out?"

"Exactly," Hazel pressed. "And why did Mr. Henry go outside at all? To meet someone? He was with Mrs. Alice when we entered. I was right behind them!"

"So, any member of our group could be the murderer," Belinda concluded thoughtfully, "assuming, of course, it wasn't a local villager with a grudge against tourists."

"But there are at least two people who were

likely outside at the time of the murder. Jenny…" Hazel's voice trailed off, her mind racing with possibilities. "Jenny making the phone call, if she ever did, and we can't ignore Gino our driver. What do we know about him?"

"There's a third," said Belinda, "we also can't overlook Obadiah."

CHAPTER NINETEEN

The charabanc glided smoothly through the quiet streets surrounding Nohant, finally weaving past a quaint little cemetery, its weathered headstones half-hidden beneath a cloak of autumn leaves. As the vehicle came to a gentle stop at the ornate iron gates of the Maison de George Sand, there was an unusual tranquillity in the air.

Nearby, the Church of Saint-Anne loomed, while the grim stone cross stood before it, still marked with the dried blood of Mr. Henry. Swathes of red-and-white POLICE NATIONALE barrier tape fluttered in the light breeze, resembling the eerie remnants of a village festival gone awry—a stark reminder those disembarking from the vehicle were now unwitting suspects in a murder investigation.

Gino, the driver, exited the charabanc with an air of reluctant duty and swung the gate wide for the group. They emerged hesitantly, forming a wary cluster as Jenny Forrest rifled through her tour guide, searching for details about the fabled mansion ahead. The village was enveloped in an unsettling silence, its streets seemingly deserted. Belinda felt a chill run down her spine at the thought that perhaps the villagers watched from behind drawn curtains, like spectators at a grim execution, waiting for the final act before returning to their lives, relieved that the threat had been eradicated.

"Where are our American friends, Joan and Walton?" Belinda whispered, nudging Hazel with mild concern.

Hazel shrugged, casting a dismissive glance back at the charabanc. "It seems Joan has succumbed to an attack of the vapours. She sees us all as potential murderers, so she's taken to her bed, refusing to leave until she can flee back to the safety of Chicago, which is rather what the frying pan said to the kettle."

With just ZeZe and Andre remaining, the diminished group set off behind Jenny as they traversed the gates and followed the meandering pathway toward the Maison. "As the police require us to stay in the area, I propose we stretch the tour over a few days instead of trying to cram everything into one," Jenny announced, her tone firm yet oddly monotonous. "Today, let's focus in detail on the gardens. We can explore the house and its surroundings tomorrow or the next day. Given our circumstances, we've been granted easy access to the Maison."

"It hardly seems worth it with just the four of us," Hazel muttered, doubt written across her face.

"But we've paid for it," Belinda insisted, her eyes shiny with curiosity. "We might as well get our money's worth. Besides, I want to see what ZeZe is up to with her camera team."

Hazel nodded in agreement. "And what about Andre and his 'heart of Poland'? He hasn't said a word to me since Beauvais when that was all he could talk about."

Jenny's voice interrupted their thoughts.

"The French State purchased the home and garden of writer George Sand, and it features a delightful 18th-century French garden, a romantic English garden, a garden draped in climbing roses, and a sanctuary of aromatic plants and towering cedar trees—all meticulously restored to reflect their appearance during her lifetime. There's an avenue leading through a park to a tranquil lake." Her words, delivered in a flat monotone, seemed to hang in the air, threatening to induce slumber in anyone listening.

Belinda and Hazel wandered toward the English Garden, where they observed both ZeZe and Andre, their attention seemingly unfazed by Jenny's commentary, drifting toward the Maison. ZeZe began softly recording a message into her phone's microphone, her brow slightly furrowed with concentration, while Andre edged closer to the facade of the building. He inspected the windows with a curious intensity, as if he were searching for something he had lost.

Belinda glanced at Hazel, "It looks like ZeZe is dictating a treatise," she remarked dryly.

The stimulating colours of Asters and Cosmos around them failed to lure the two women further. With a shared glance, they strolled out of the garden and approached the Maison. "Let's see what Andre is up to," Hazel suggested, a playful glint in her eye.

Andre, deep in his inspection, was oblivious to their approach. He moved to the rear of the building, where the windows were shuttered tight. With a touch of desperation, he rattled the shutters, hoping to find one that would yield to his touch.

"Breaking and entering is a crime in any country," Hazel said loudly.

Startled, Andre turned to them, his cheeks flushing crimson, betraying a mix of surprise and embarrassment. "I just…" he stammered, fumbling for words.

Hazel chuckled, "Don't worry, your secret is safe with us."

Andre coughed, managing a somewhat sheepish smile. "I'm in your debt. I was just checking… on the security." There was little conviction in his words, and the tension hung palpably in the air.

"A good thing," Belinda replied, "I'm sure there are countless national treasures inside." He sensed the scepticism in her voice and frowned. "Yes, and I trust we will soon be able to see them." With a nod, he briskly walked back, the women trailing behind him.

"A security check, my pert derriere," said Hazel, shaking her head. "He was casing the joint."

"That certainly looked like it," Belinda agreed, her brows furrowing in thought. "But why?"

As they approached the central courtyard, a wayward cloud drifted overhead, casting a shadow that transformed the pale stone building into a more sinister version of its intended elegance. There stood Gino, leaning casually against a tree, puffing on a particularly pungent cigarette. His eyes darted between them, Andre, and ZeZe, a flicker of intrigue in his gaze. Unbeknownst to them, they were also being watched from a hidden vantage point—Obadiah, lurking in the shadows, raised his phone to capture their every move.

CHAPTER TWENTY

The morning sun struggled to break through the heavy mist that enveloped the landscape, casting a sombre hue over the chapel where Belinda and Hazel found themselves at breakfast. It was just the two of them at the long, wooden table that creaked softly with their every movement. There was no sign of ZeZe and Andre, and it seemed Walter and Joan had barricaded themselves in their cell, likely too terrified to face the day, lest the bogeyman emerge to claim them. The waitress, a petite figure wrapped in a simple uniform, glided over to their table. She wore an expression that seemed to mirror the weight of the atmosphere. "Miss Forrest has been called to the police station in Châteauroux," she informed them, her voice just above a whisper. "I was instructed to tell you that the tour will be delayed and resumed tomorrow."

A flash of irritation flickered across Hazel's face as she shot back, "And what are we supposed to do in the meantime?" Her impatience filled the room. The waitress offered only a non-committal shrug before she set a heavy coffee jug on the table, as if it contained a possible suggestion, then turned and vanished into what was once the entrance to a confessional, a reminder of secrets and sins.

Belinda's mind was already racing ahead. "We can take another look at Nohant Maison," she suggested, her tone shifting to one of resolve as she poured steaming coffee into two mismatched cups.

"And don't forget about the small cemetery on the grounds. I want to check that out. Mr. Henry was attacked with what the police believe to be part of a headstone, it might be linked to that place."

"More than likely," Hazel conceded reluctantly, her practicality surfacing. "But it's cold, and those clouds overhead promise rain." With a glimmer of defiance, Belinda responded, "So we rug up and take umbrellas. Or would you prefer to spend the day in the Priory contemplating your sins?" The thought of trapping herself indoors, with the weight of unresolved mysteries pressing down, held very little charm for Hazel. A day spent brooding would only heighten her sense of dread. "Alright, but if I catch pneumonia, you're footing the hospital bills," she replied, a hint of reluctance still in her tone.

With borrowed umbrellas in tow, they set out toward the Maison de George Sand. The enveloping mist added an otherworldly quality to their journey, wrapping the landscape in mystery. More than once, they ventured off the path, colliding with wooden fences and stumbling over hidden potholes. The open fields lay barren, the round hay bales looming like ghostly sentinels shrouded in fog. The air was still, devoid of the usual morning symphony of birdsong, making the crunch of their footsteps the only testament to life in this dreary expanse.

"Why Mr. Henry?" Hazel's sudden question broke through Belinda's contemplative silence, pulling her back to the urgency of their predicament.

"Why kill him, you mean?" Belinda asked, caught off guard for a moment by the straightforwardness of the inquiry.

"What was it about him that warranted his murder?" Hazel pressed, her brows furrowed.

"He was a film producer. So is his sister, Mrs. Alice," Belinda rationalized, carefully avoiding another pothole as she spoke. "Perhaps they had enemies lurking in Hollywood—mafia types with vendettas."

Hazel grunted in response, her disbelief evident. "Well deserved, judging by the type of films they produced. But it's hard to believe anyone in our little group is a studio fixer in mufti."

"Which brings us back to the crux of the matter: Who is the murderer and why?" Belinda replied, but Hazel interrupted. "What about ZeZe? She's making a film or some sort of documentary, remember? You saw her with a camera crew back in Beauvais."

"If Mr. Henry and Alice were also filming, maybe they were collaborating on a project?" speculated Belinda, glancing at the thickening clouds above.

"Which would be what, exactly?" Hazel queried, the intrigue evident in her voice. Belinda shrugged, her mind racing. "Presumably something based in France. Perhaps exploring the life of George Sand or their interpretation of it?"

"Or Chopin," Hazel countered thoughtfully.

"And our Polish friend, Andre, seems particularly obsessed with Chopin."

"Exactly," Belinda replied, her curiosity piqued. "If Andre believed that Mr. Henry was planning a project that might portray Chopin unfairly—or disrespectfully—he just might want him out of the way."

"But if that's the case, Mrs Alice could be next on the list," Hazel cautioned, her eyes narrowing as the implications settled in.

"Hmmm... but what about the others? Let's not forget about ZeZe's film," Belinda mused aloud. "When I saw her taping, she was babbling in French. The only word I caught was Disneyland."

"And she was recording something in French on her phone yesterday. But I can't draw any connections between George Sand, Chopin, and Disneyland," Hazel said, frowning as she wrestled with the maze of possibilities. "And even if there was a connection, what could it possibly have to do with Mr. Henry's murder?"

"Perhaps we can dismiss Walter and Joan as suspects," Belinda suggested, "but that leaves us with Jenny and Gino, our driver. What could motivate a tour guide and a driver to commit murder, especially someone they haven't even met until they joined the tour?"

"But we don't know that for sure," Hazel countered, shaking her head. "And we can't rule out Obadiah. So far he's the chief looney in this particular Bedlam we've stumbled into. What do we really know about him? Did he have any previous contact with Mr. Henry?"

As their footsteps began to falter under the weight of exhaustion, the village emerged from its mysterious shroud in the distance, guiding them towards the graveyard. The small, rustic cemetery came into view, nestled amongst ancient trees, witnesses to secrets of the past. As they approached the Sand family section, pockets of lingering fog clung to headstones and crosses, adding an air of melancholia to the scene.

"Damn," Hazel exclaimed suddenly, her face twisting in discomfort. "I shouldn't have had that second cup of coffee. I need to find a restroom." Belinda shot a glance towards the Maison, considering their options. "Maybe they have facilities for tourists. If not, there are plenty of bushes in the garden that could serve as temporary cover."

"Right," Hazel sighed, a note of urgency creeping into her voice. "If I'm not back in half an hour, send out a Saint Bernard with a gin and tonic." With a determined nod, she hurried off in search of relief, leaving Belinda alone amidst the sombre stones.

Standing in the graveyard, Belinda looked around the melancholy setting. At her feet, a stone cherub lay, its once delicate wings now broken, and its head missing—an eerie sight that sent a shiver down her spine. A strand of red and white police barrier tape lay gracefully across the fallen angel.

In that moment, the realization struck her. The stone head was the murder weapon used to kill Mr. Henry. The surprising revelation unnerved her as she moved toward the large, raised grey stone tomb of George Sand, nestled closely to the gnarled trunk of an enormous overshadowing tree. From her vantage point, the towering form of the Church of St. Anne stood proudly, a silent witness to the unfolding drama encasing the village.

A shiver ran down Belinda's spine. She half-turned, as the sound of footsteps echoed through the mist, sending a ripple of unease through her.

"Hazel? Did you—" she began, but her words caught in her throat. With a sudden, instinctive movement, she completed the turn. There, just a short distance away, a tall, dark figure loomed, its silhouette sharply defined against the shadows..

An unnerving presence.

CHAPTER TWENTY-ONE

"G'day."

Faced with a spectre as she stood amid the ice-cold stones of the graveyard, the last thing Belinda expected was an Australian greeting.

"Sorry, I didn't mean to scare you," the voice continued, soothing yet filled with an unmistakable lilt of mischief. The figure stepped closer. Belinda allowed herself to breathe a little easier. Before her appeared a young man, tall and slender, clutching a video camera, the lens glinting dully amidst the shadows. However, she remained wary, acutely aware of her surroundings as the forbidding tombstones loomed around her and the iron fence loomed even higher.

"I'm just taking some videos of the house and gardens," he explained, a hint of enjoyment colouring his voice.

"Oh," Belinda replied, attempting to mask her anxiety. "I'm just a visitor too."

The man broke into a wide smile, the kind that could light up the gloomiest of days. "You're an Aussie? What are the odds? Our accent is a dead giveaway. Hi, I'm Barry McDonald."

Belinda furrowed her brow, a sense of familiarity washing over her. "Bazza?"

He chuckled, shaking his head in playful denial. "Macca."

A smile crept across Belinda's lips. "I should have known. I'm Belinda Lawrence."

"Mmm, Sydney?" he guessed, sparkling with curiosity.

"Never," she replied. "Melbourne."

Macca nodded knowingly. "Perth for me. But I spent my film school days in Melbourne."

"What brings you to Nohant?" Belinda inquired, studying him with keen interest—his tanned skin and tousled hair suggested a life spent catching waves.

"Oh, just for work," Macca said nonchalantly. "I ditched film school. Too many wankers, so I hopped over to Europe. Scored a gig with an agency in London, making videos that allow me to travel and get paid."

Belinda raised an eyebrow. "So why Nohant?"

"I'm doing a promo video for a client. A French woman—some kind of tour," he explained.

It all clicked into place for Belinda. "Would that be ZeZe Dupont?"

Macca's face lit up with recognition. "That's right! I thought you looked familiar. You were near that Cathedral, Saint-Pierre in Beauvais, after we wrapped up the interview with ZeZe. I noticed you standing there."

Hazel tried to remember the last time her knees had been this close to her face. Aside from any emotional tangle, she felt certain it was some years past during a riotous evening in Cannes at The Carlton, when after her fifth Martini, she had been encouraged to join a group in a game of Twister.

That now, was a faint memory but the current reality was the cramped space in the back seat of a Tin Snail hurtling along a country road. With every jolt, her head collided with the sagging canvas roof of what she believed to be the first ever off the assembly line at the Citroën DS factory in the last century. Trying to catch a glimpse of the front seats, she eyed the back of Belinda's head and that of the chattering Australian. "Do you think it's possible to drive a tad more sedately?" Hazel asked, her voice tinged with irritation.

Macca glanced over with an apologetic grin. "Sorry! This old bomb of a Citroën has a mind of its own." Belinda, seated beside him, clutched the edge of her seat. "Why did you buy this scrap heap?" Macca laughed heartily. "Not me! I borrowed it from a mate for the shoot." The ancient car skidded around another corner. "I doubt there will be anything left to return to him," Belinda said, her apprehension barely masked. "It won't be long now. We're nearly in Sarzay. I hear there's an excellent café there. Perfect for lunch," Macca assured her, his enjoyment palpable. From the rear seat, Hazel interjected with annoyance. "I hope it has a bar!"

Lunch unfolded beneath the expansive, ivy-clad façade of the café, the reluctant sun piercing through the thinning mists, casting a gentle warmth over the reserved group. As they settled at the weathered outdoor table, Belinda and Macca engaged in lively chatter, sharing anecdotes of their homeland and marvelling at the quirky nuances of the English and French cultures. After indulging in a decadent chocolate pudding, they sank into a contented silence, savouring the moment. Taking advantage of their lull, Hazel coughed delicately, her curiosity getting the better of her.

"Belinda tells me you were filming a video about ZeZe. What is it all about?"

Macca shrugged, a bemused expression crossing his face. "Beats me."

"But you must have some insight," Belinda pressed, her brows furrowing slightly. "You've been recording her throughout the tour."

"True," Macca admitted, his expression shifting to one of mild frustration. "But she spoke French the whole time. I didn't understand a word. All I did was video her."

"Not a single word?" Hazel asked, disbelief etching her features.

"Okay, maybe one or two here and there. Just names like Nohant, George Sand, you know, stuff that relates to the tour. Oh, and Disneyland. She mentioned that." He wore a puzzled look, scratching his head. "I'm still not sure what she meant by that."

"Disneyland?" Hazel echoed, intrigue piquing.

Macca chuckled to himself. "Maybe she expected Donald Duck to drop by for a visit."

A shared silence fell over the trio as each one conjured their comical visions of animated chaos. Belinda leaned forward, placing her hand on Macca's arm in earnest. "What about your mate, the one with the microphone?"

Macca snorted with laughter. "Unlucky Pierre?"

"Unlucky? How so?" Belinda said.

"With the ladies, he's got no luck at all," Macca replied, with a wink.

"Be that as it may," Belinda said, her tone grave, "he recorded everything ZeZe said. He must have some idea of her intentions."

Macca shrugged. "I suppose, he is French."

"Where is he now?" Hazel pressed, her interest intensifying.

"Off on another job, I think. ZeZe wrapped up her spoken commentary for the video. I'm just capturing B-roll footage now," Macca explained.

"Do you have his phone number?" Belinda asked urgently. Macca nodded, sensing the shift in tension. "Why is it so important to know what she's up to?"

"Macca," Belinda's voice turned serious, "a man has been murdered. Everyone on our tour is a suspect. ZeZe doesn't seem like your average tourist. Why have you follow her? Can you ring Pierre?"

Macca looked at her and realised she was in earnest. "OK. I'll give him a bell." He reached for his phone, punched in a number and waited. A reedy French voice answered. With his phone to his ear, Macca rose and sauntered off, "Pierre, G'day mate, it's Macca. Got a question for you." He drifted away leaving Belinda and Hazel in a state of heightened anticipation.

CHAPTER TWENTY-TWO

Andre hurried into the Church of Saint-Anne and sat as though seeking sanctuary. Slightly breathless from recent activity he welcomed the calm. He pulled his hand from his pocket and removed a blood-stained handkerchief. The small cut on his hand had stopped bleeding. He rewound the cloth and covered the wound. He knew there would be activity at the Maison; the shriek of a Security Alarm penetrating the late afternoon had certainly alerted the village. As if on cue, he heard the excited babble of female voices. Rising, he moved to the door making sure he could not be seen. A group of four women stood at the gates to Nohant gesticulating excitedly. No doubt this intrusion would take its place in the historical fabric of village life over the next few decades.

Another noise joined the hubbub. A police siren. Andre sank back into the gloom of the interior, produced his camera and began to photograph the ancient wall paintings. After all, he was just a tourist. Outside, a police car made a leisurely addition to the tableau at the gates. Andre's curiosity got the better of him. He sought the shadows at the door again. Two young policemen advanced towards the women and, confronted with wild gesticulations and chatter, were more or less informed of the tragedy unfolding in the Maison. Acknowledging the women and presenting themselves as superior males, they opened the gates and disappeared behind the building.

Andre felt it safe to appear. Strolling across the square, wounded hand hidden in a pocket, camera in the other, he approached the women. All four turned curious eyes towards him.

"Bon après midi. Mówisz po polsku?"

Three women drew back from him, but the fourth, a generation younger and certainly more attractive replied,

"Non. Français ou anglaise."

"Ah," said Andre. "That is good. I wonder what has happened. What are the police doing?"

Three of the women looked at him with deepening suspicion. The younger woman smiled. It was good to see new blood in the village. "There has been a break in at the Maison."

"Oh, that is terrible. Has anything been stolen?"

"Maybe. Maybe not," said the woman indifferently.

"I hope not," said Andre with a smile. "I'm a tourist and we are due to see the interior sometime soon."

"I hope that we will see more of you in Nohant," was the woman's reply, with more ambiguity than was required, "but we are cautious as there has been a murder, and strangers are under suspicion."

Andre smiled to himself nodded to the women and turned away. As he walked he could feel judgmental eyes on him, six critical, two shameless. His path took him towards the nearby graveyard and a sudden movement amid the gravestones caught his attention. He paused; his curiosity aroused. The figure flitted between light and shade. It was only as the shape was disappearing into the dark that a memory was triggered. A memory which raised more questions than answers. It was Obadiah James.

CHAPTER TWENTY-THREE

ZeZe glanced up from her laptop. On the screen her image in the interview videoed in Beauvais continued to play but her attention was elsewhere. Automatically she selected a chocolate from the nearby box and savoured her favourite Truffle addiction. A glance out the window from her room in the Priory hotel intensified when the distant figure of Andre came into view. She watched as he made his way to the entrance. He had clearly been out walking. But where to? There was only one answer to that. The Maison. And why? Again, a simple answer. She recalled the time the guide girl, Jenny had taken them to visit the exterior. Andre had left the group and had ventured to the rear of the building. No doubt he was seeking entrance. Entrance that was to be unnoticed and permit him to carry out his search undisturbed. No doubt he had attempted to gain entry again today. Had he been successful? His demeanour indicated not. Her attention drifted back to the computer screen, but her thoughts remained on Andre. If he was successful with his search and found what he was seeking, did it present problems for her and her plans? There had to be a way to circumvent any difficulty. She would let nothing get in her way.

"Disneyland?"
Macca shook his head. "No, she said it *wasn't* like Disneyland."

"Well what did Piere, unlucky or not, tell you?" said Belinda.

Driving along the way to the Priory hotel, Macca swerved to avoid a wayward rabbit.. "His English is not too good, but from what he could understand from the interviews it seems ZeZe plans to open a Theme Park, or more accurately a Theme Village."

"Where?" grunted Hazel from the back seat.

Macca nodded out the window. "Here. In Nohant. She wants to take over the village and convert the cottages into guest houses."

"When you say, Theme Village," said Belinda, "what's the theme?"

"From what Pierre said, it was centred on Nohant. George Sand, Chopin, but also included Edith Wharton and Henry James, who visited in their old motor car."

"I don't get it," said Belinda.

"I think I have an idea of what she plans," said Hazel, shifting unsuccessfully into a less cramped position. "Have festivals celebrating their lives."

"More or less but a bit more. There will be concerts of Chopin's music, readings by famous people of Sand's works. Same applies to Edith and Henry. People would come to the village, stay in a cottage, attend the festivities, and eat at local restaurants. A whole arty experience."

"And presumably pay a lot for the experience," said Belinda.

"I doubt ZeZe is the charitable sort," said

Hazel.

"Anything else?" said Belinda.

Macca pulled the Citroën up to a shuddering halt, testing the sustainability of the chassis. "I think there's more, but I'll have to ring Pierre again. He did mention something about what was in the interior of the Maison...hair, or something."

Belinda and Hazel unwound themselves from the vehicle and stood at the entrance to the hotel. "I'll give you a bell tomorrow after I have a yarn with Pierre," said Macca as he started the car, but brought it to an abrupt stop, with the accompanying clatter of loose metal.

"I remember what was in the Maison that is important. A heart." With that he rattled away.

Belinda and Hazel looked at each other. "A heart?"

CHAPTER TWENTY-FOUR

Mrs Alice sat in the back of the police car as it left the hospital in Châteauroux. Her return to Nohant and the group she knew would cause comment. They would expect her to immediately return to Los Angeles with Henry's mortal remains. Not continue a tourist excursion. She glanced down at the Louis Vuitton case and the brown cardboard box on the seat beside her. Henry had always been tall; strange he now amounted to a pile of dust in a container the size of a tissue box. He could remain with her until her return to Los Angeles. No sense wasting money on postage. Finally he provided a reason to open the plot they had chosen in Hollywood Forever Cemetery. She was beginning to think it was a waste of money. Henry's autopsy had proved nothing else but the blow to his head as the cause of his death. Prostate and liver complaints might have eventually carried him off, but it seems he met an early death, or at least so the Coroner claimed. The police had interrogated her and the members of the group but came to no conclusion. There didn't seem to be any motive for doing away with Henry, and the judiciary was of the opinion the perpetrator was a passing vagrant who thought he could steal valuables from Henry. An isolated case. Mrs Alice formed the opinion the police welcomed this view and were content to deal with the usual village misdemeanours. 'Ne faites pas de vagues'.
The passing countryside held no attraction as

Mrs Alice's thoughts were firmly fixed on her companions in the group.

Had ZeZe progressed with her plans to turn Nohant into a tourist trap? It went against the woman's role as an activist preserving French history, but chicanery and cunning could keep her as a silent partner, while her public image would remain as the Saint Joan for preservation of Gallic antiquity, untouched by sordid commercial revenue. Not the first social figure to profit by subterfuge.

Commercial revenue was uppermost in Mrs Alice's mind. Now Henry had passed, she would continue to video every aspect of Nohant in preparation of the Pitch Deck she was preparing.

Her mind wandered. That Pole...Andre Levinz? How did he fit in? The two women, the Australian and the older English woman, appeared to be tourists. But one can never tell. She gave no thought to the young American couple. ZeZe wormed her way back into her thoughts. Time was of the essence, and it would be a race to see who raised the finance first to enable work to begin on either project. If ZeZe won, Mrs Alice knew her plans would be in ruins.

The police car made its way through Nohant and passed the Church of Saint-Anne. She noted the Police barrier tape was still clinging to the Cross. Would the group accept the theory it was a passing stranger who murdered Henry? Or did they have suspicions as to who in the group was a killer?

CHAPTER TWENTY-FIVE

The cheery yellow charabanc drew to a stop at the gates of the Maison Nohant its cheerful colour the only note of optimism in the muted morning light. It held a full contingent of those remaining on the Motor Flight Tour. Mrs Alice had been greeted with sympathy on the loss of Mr Henry and had accepted that compassion with a mixture of acceptance and privately held scepticism, after all, there had been an unsolved murder.

"As I told you earlier," said Jenny as the group left the vehicle, "even though the police think Mr Henry was killed by a vagrant, we have been asked to remain in Nohant for the immediate future. It will allow us to continue on here for the allotted scheduled days and beyond. The only clue found at the scene is the leather glove which held the murder weapon. Apparently there is a mixture of DNA within it, which is why we were asked to have an oral swab from the inside of our cheeks. Police used a Rapid DNA system which gave a quick result and proved to be negative. Now if you follow me, we will begin the interior tour of the Maison."

She watched each member closely as they passed by her, Walter and Joan bringing up the rear. Apparently their hotel room had become too claustrophobic, they had belief in the police's theory and considered it safe to mix with their tour companions again.

The group entered the Vestibule and stood

sheeplike until Jenny took control. "We will begin the tour in the Salon." So saying she moved to a room on the right and shepherded them in. "This is one of my favorite rooms. Original tapestry and portraits of ancestors are displayed here, along with a portrait of George Sand by Auguste Charpentier. Evenings would be spent here playing games or watching a puppet show."

The group responded in various ways as Jenny continued description of the many items on display. Belinda was distracted as she saw ZeZe step aside from the others and quietly begin to record something on her phone microphone. Recalling that ZeZe had done something similar on their first visit to the gardens, Belinda assumed she was recording details of the interiors for her Video. A movement near the doorway into the Vestibule caught her eye and she was surprised to see Macca, camera in hand, making his way into a room opposite. Separating herself quietly from the others who seemed to hang on Jenny's every word, Belinda stepped across the Vestibule and into the other room. Macca looked up as she entered. "G'day. I was hoping I'd see you here."

"What are you doing," said Belinda, glancing over her shoulder to see if anyone had seen her leave.

"Shooting some interiors for ZeZe's video. Listen, I've got something to tell you. I rang Pierre again and it seems that at some time while we were filming her, ZeZe told him of a tale related to Chopin, who you know lived here with George. Seems when he died he was buried in Père-Lachaise Cemetery in Paris, but his heart was sent to Warsaw where it was placed in a memorial in a church."

"So what's the tale?"

Macca glanced cautiously around in a conspiratorial manner. "The story is the heart in Warsaw is not genuine and Chopin's real heart is hidden here in the Maison."

CHAPTER TWENTY-SIX

"Well, that explains Andre's interest," said Hazel, "he went on about something of importance to Poland being at Nohant whatever it was, but was Poland's heart, or something similar."

"Meaning Chopin's heart," said Belinda.

Strolling back to the hotel seemed a good way to assess the latest development. They watched the group drive off in the charabanc.

"So let's put this together," continued Belinda, as she glanced back at George Sand's tomb, "it seems ZeZe has heard this story and if true, how does it affect her plans for a theme village?"

"A plus or a minus?" said Hazel,

"Assume it's a plus, and Andre comes along and maybe wants to remove it to Warsaw, if the heart there isn't the real one."

"So it's removed and is one less selling point in ZeZe's plans."

"So it's in her favour if indeed the heart is here and remains here," said Belinda.

"Assuming of course the Polish Government would even consider that happening. Also, it would have to be proved that the Nohant heart is either genuine or a fake," said Hazel.

"And the same with the Warsaw heart," said Belinda, "which brings us back to Andre and who is he and what proof does he have it is not genuine. And the real one is here in Nohant?"

They strolled on in a silence broken by Hazel.

"In the middle of all this is Obadiah and the police don't have his DNA to match it to the murderer's glove."

CHAPTER TWENTY-SEVEN

Obadiah watched the charabanc leave the Maison with Belinda and Hazel following on foot. From the cottage window close by the Church of Saint-Anne he'd been observing their activity since their morning arrival at Nohant, as he had on previous occasions. He sank back on the bed, removed his wire frame glasses, polished them with the edge of the rustic Couvre-lit and reviewed his situation. He had to admit to himself he had been foolish to leave the tour at Amiens and in such a dramatic way. But he had made such a fool of himself at the dining room by asking Andre such a stupid question. Why did he think a Pole could supply details of Morton Fullerton and Uncle Henry? And rushing like that from the room. A petulant schoolboy. He'd been uncomfortable with all the strangers in the foreign environment and panicked. Wondering if he'd made the right decision in taking the tour. Even now his cheeks flushed more than their normal pink as he recalled his embarrassment. They must think him a fool. Alone later in the hotel room, his humiliation had grown to be unbearable, and it was impossible to face the group again. His midnight flight from the hotel which left him wandering the dark streets in a foreign town in a foreign country only added to the nightmare.

The surreal journey provided by a farmer in

offering him a lift in his huge tractor, had brought him within a few miles of Nohant. Driving through the night his saviour at the wheel, who fortunately spoke some English, showed no interest in the traveller, an American from somewhere named Caroline du Nor, nor surprise he should be roaming the countryside dressed as for an evening at home. Proclaiming he was Jean- Baptiste, the farmer, for the remainder of the journey, spilled a torrent of abuse on corrupt local Councils and cheating grocery chains, all in smouldering French. It was the pungent smell preceding the two bright headlights and the roar of the tractor that added to the terrors of the black night. A trailer laden with manure, hay, and rotten fruit and a large container of well-aged liquid manure, added a malodorous supplement to the rage Jean-Baptiste dumped on one of the many planned targets for the pungent cargo. Indeed Obadiah had absorbed some of the stench which clung to him for several days. Luckily it had passed before he was able to visit the Maison as a tourist. If it had remained he thought the locals would have their suspicions about Les Américains confirmed.

With sudden alarm he instantly felt in his shirt pocket. His passport and bank card were secure. He offered a prayer of thanks that he'd had the good sense to have them when he fled. Finding accommodation in a guest house in Nohant had been a surprise. He regretted the loss of his suitcase and the research documents on Fullerton and Uncle

Henry...there was a chance they had travelled with the group and were held at the Saint-Chartier Priory. And he feared losing Frankie, his most treasured companion. He'd ventured several times to reclaim them but at the last-minute shame overcame him and he returned crestfallen to his small dwelling in Nohant. He put on his glasses and returned to the window. Frustration overwhelmed him as he knew how close he was to the spirits. And of course, there was the murder.

CHAPTER TWENTY-EIGHT

Andre reclined in the charabanc, feeling the warm sun seep through the window as they made their way to the Priory. Despite the pleasant surroundings, a cloud of frustration hung over him.

The morning had been less than productive, marred by the unexpected restrictions placed upon the exploration of the Maison by Jenny. She had made it abundantly clear that, over the next few days, they would meticulously comb through each and every room, methodically cataloguing their findings until the police granted them the freedom to move on. This deliberate pace was exasperating for Andre, who felt an urgent need to delve deeper into the core of his quest. He had become singularly obsessed with the idea of discovering Chopin's heart, convinced that it might still lie hidden within the Maison's enigmatic walls. Yet his belief was not universally shared; his colleagues back in Warsaw had openly ridiculed his assertions, pointing out that Chopin had wished for his heart to be returned to Poland. However, a captivating notion had seized Andre's imagination: what if George Sand, the famed romantic of Chopin's life, had kept the heart, substituting it with another before sending it away? This theory had burgeoned into an obsession, a tantalizing mystery that he felt compelled to unravel.

As the charabanc's tires rumbled over the cobblestones, his mind flicked back over the past few days in a torrent of memories. He recalled with a start the day he had tried to clandestinely enter the Maison, the thrill of risk coursing through him, followed by the disconcerting sight of a shadowy figure—Obadiah—scurrying away in what seemed like a panic. The memory chilled him; had the man seen him attempt to break in? He pondered this as they rolled along, a knot of worry tightening in his stomach. If Obadiah had indeed witnessed his failed endeavour, it would be best for all involved if the man chose to remain silent about it.

CHAPTER TWENTY-NINE

In the Priory garden, Hazel's voice sliced through the tranquil ambiance. "Now we know what is driving ZeZe and Andre—a heart that may or may not be here, yet it holds immense value for both parties. It might even be significant to Mrs. Alice if she intends to make a film showing the shenanigans that went on in the Maison. So my question to you is, how does the murder of Mr. Henry fit into this unfolding drama? A real commedia dell'arte?" Hazel brushed a fallen leaf from her lap, her fingers lingering on the vibrant scarlet and gold hues of autumn. The bench she occupied was surrounded by a riot of colour, the air fragrant with the mingled scents of late blooms and moist earth.

"It's merely our speculation that Mrs. Alice is planning a film," Belinda replied, her brow furrowed in thought, "but you really don't subscribe to the police's theory that the murderer was just a vagrant lingering near the Priory, do you?"

"And neither do you," Hazel countered swiftly. "If that were the case, they'd let us go without a second thought." Belinda pondered this for a moment, her gaze drifting to the garden's well-manicured hedges. "A film could jeopardize ZeZe's carefully crafted vision for the tourist village," she ventured cautiously.

"Or it could do quite the opposite," Hazel interjected frostily. "A grand Hollywood production could spotlight Nohant, exposing it to the masses—

modern audiences, of course, will likely twist its history to suit their tastes, reducing it to simplistic rubbish that even a three-year-old could grasp, unaware of the world beyond their own street."

"Where's Ken Russell when you need him," said Belinda.

Hazel nodded slowly, her eyes narrowing. "Or indeed Mr. Henry." She contemplated the implications further. "If either ZeZe or Andre perceived him and Mrs. Alice as a threat, it could very well be the case of 'one down, one to go.'"

"So, you're suggesting the murderer could potentially be either ZeZe or Andre?" Belinda asked, her voice steady but laced with tension.

"Let's not forget—Mrs. Alice may be a Deadman walking," Hazel replied, her tone darkening.

The serene atmosphere of the garden was shattered by the arrival of a cacophonous noise. The rattles, bangs, and clanking echoed ominously, signalling the arrival of Macca in his notoriously primal Citroën.

"G'day, ladies!" Macca called, his vibrant personality filling the space. "I'm heading off to the UK for a few days. Got a gig in Durham for a photo shoot, but I'll be back before you know it. In the meantime, you can take the car if you need to get around." Belinda felt her stomach churn at the mention of the rust bucket she had dubbed "the rolling disaster."

"Thanks a lot," she managed, her voice laced

with doubt.

"I'm being picked up and taken straight to the airport. I'll be back in a few days!" As a taxi pulled into the grounds, Macca turned back to Belinda. "Take care of it, it's precious to my mate." With a wave, he hopped into the waiting taxi, disappearing from sight.

As night fell, the air became surprisingly balmy, a gentle breeze rustling through the trees. Moonlight spilled into the tiny cell that served as Belinda's temporary home within the converted Priory. The peacefulness enveloped her, yet her mind raced with an array of unsettling thoughts surrounding not only the murder of Mr. Charles but the entire concept of the motor flight and the diverse individuals embarking on that peculiar tour. All she sought were answers, but they remained elusive, shrouded in an intricate web of mystery. Tossing back her covers, Belinda flicked on the light, donning a robe she ventured into the dimly lit hallway. Perhaps a stroll in the night air would provide clarity. She descended to the lower level, poised to continue her path when a cell door creaked open nearby. Her eyes widened as she caught a glimpse of ZeZe, her face animated as she whispered in hushed tones to a companion. The door swung shut, and in the faint light, Belinda recognized the wiry, familiar shape of Gino, the mute boxer. He paused, then moved stealthily to a cell at the far end of the corridor. With three soft raps on the door, it creaked open, light spilling forth as Gino stepped inside. The door clicked shut behind him. Straining to listen, Belinda leaned closer, holding her breath as she distinctly heard Jenny's authoritative voice pierce the stillness. Yet she was astonished to detect a reply—a male voice, urgent and raspy. But Gino was a mute; how could this be happening?

"You were drunk," Hazel accused, her tone teasing yet laced with a hint of seriousness as she nursed a steaming cup of coffee. Belinda put her cup down with a flourish, a hint of indignation in her voice. "I was not drunk."

"Last night, you looked like you were judging a Gin Festival," Hazel remarked, a smile creeping onto her lips.

"Two martinis, tops! That was just to steel my nerve for the test drive of Macca's Citroën around the car park," Belinda said, her voice rising slightly in defence.

"Which you actually managed quite well—though, regrettably, it didn't end well for the flower bed," Hazel pointed out,.

"Accidents will happen," Belinda shrugged, an airy dismissal of the disaster. "Besides, if I were you, I'd be wary of throwing gin accusations around. Too close to home, wouldn't you agree? But what's important is that Gino was speaking. Engaging in conversation with Jenny...and likely with ZeZe."

Hazel glanced around the nearly empty breakfast room, noting the last lingering guest finally depart. "If what you say is true, then why maintain the facade of being mute?" she mused, brow furrowing in contemplation.

"And at whose bidding?" Belinda added, her curiosity piqued. "It seems like both ZeZe and Jenny are involved in something larger. But for what purpose?"

"Assuming there was no other man present," Hazel continued thoughtfully, "and that it was indeed Gino, he could very well serve as a conduit for the two women."

"A spy, you mean?" Belinda raised an eyebrow, intrigued. "But who is he spying on, and why?"

"If the value of Chopin's true heart turning up here at Nohant is as substantial as rumoured, and it holds significance for all three contenders—ZeZe, Andre, and Mrs. Alice—it's certain that ZeZe will wield whatever influence she possesses to grasp it firmly in her diamond encrusted fingers."

CHAPTER THIRTY

Andre paused at the noble gates of the Maison, his heart racing with anticipation and a hint of trepidation. The police's directive for the group to linger longer than initially planned while they probed the mystery surrounding Mr. Henry's murder was unexpectedly advantageous for him. It granted him additional opportunities to scour the sprawling building for Chopin's heart, which he desperately sought. However, gaining access to the inner sanctum of the Maison appeared to hinge solely on Jenny's presence, a fact that stirred his annoyance. With a determined breath, he pushed aside his frustrations and made his way into the grounds, moving toward the grand entrance of the house. As he approached, a wave of surprise washed over him; the large pale blue doors stood wide open, as if inviting him inside. His fortune seemed to be shifting. Cautiously, he stepped through the threshold and entered the Vestibule, now illuminated by soft, filtered light.

From a room ahead, he was met with the sounds of activity—a soft clattering of plates and cutlery accompanied by the gentle and enchanting humming of "La Vie en Rose," creating an ambiance that was both warm and welcoming. Curiosity piqued, Andre crossed the Vestibule and entered the Salle à Manger, the dining room. There, he found a woman diligently setting a dining table for an elaborate meal. She paused upon sensing his presence, her humming fading into silence as she turned to face him. To his astonishment, Andre recognized her instantly; she was the same woman he had encountered during his previous ill-fated attempt to break into the mansion. A flicker of recognition sparked in her eyes, and a confident, challenging smile spread across her face.

"Ah, monsieur, vous êtes rentrés, pardonnez-moi! I remember... you do not speak French, but you have returned. Was there something here that drew you back?" Her question was laced with a playful belief that nothing in Nohant could compare to her own allure.

Caught off guard by her exuberance, Andre instinctively took a half step back, trying to regain his composure. "Bonjour, we meet again. The door was open, and I was just going to inspect the rooms," he replied, attempting to sound casual.

The woman placed down a set of exquisite 19th-century French faience dinner plates, each piece delicately crafted with intricate designs, and took a few steps closer to him. "Je m'appelle Marie. I work here sometimes, doing some cleaning, helping out—ce genre de choses," she explained, her tone both inviting and familiar. Andre nodded, taking in her name. "Andre Levinz," he introduced himself, trying to match her ease.

Marie's eyes sparkled with recognition. "You are with the tourists? In the big bus?" she asked, a hint of curiosity in her voice. "No? You are coming to the fête?" She waved a hand toward the dining table adorned with fine china. A look of confusion crossed Andre's face as he processed her words. "You don't know about the feast to be held here? Have they not informed you?" Marie asked, her tone shifting to one of incredulity. "The French woman on the tour, the one who is high and mighty from Paris—she plans for you all to dine here. It will be a grand événement. Candles, music, wine."

"You mean ZeZe?" Andre inquired, a flicker of realization dawning on him. Marie shrugged, indicating her acknowledgment of the name. "It will be like Baronne Dudevant, vous la connaissez sous le nom de George Sand. Ah... wearing clothes just like she and Chopin did," she added with a knowing smile.

"In costume?" Andre responded, his surprise evident. With a playful shrug, Marie slipped into a mock seductive pose, as though she expected this kind of extravagance from city dwellers. "Monsieur will look très beau," she teased, her eyes glinting mischievously. Despite Marie's flirtation, Andre's thoughts were miles away. ZeZe's unexpected dinner gathering consumed his mind; what could her motives possibly be? Was she aware of the heart's existence in the mansion? The urgency of his mission began to weigh heavily on him.

Just then, the sound of footsteps echoed from the staircase, drawing his attention. He glanced up to see a figure descending the steps. A fleeting glimpse of ZeZe rushed through the Vestibule, her form purposeful as she darted out of the house.

Had she been searching for the heart? The sense of urgency heightened; he needed to find a way into the Maison and commence his investigation. His thoughts were abruptly interrupted by more footsteps. A new figure emerged into the hallway, halting abruptly when they spotted Andre. It was Gino, the familiar visage bringing a mix of relief and apprehension.

CHAPTER THIRTY-ONE

"Does my bum look big in this?" Hazel asked as she tied the elaborate bustle cage securely around her waist, its addition a self-evident response to her question. The intricate lace and satin fabric of her petticoat swirled around her legs as she slipped it over the top. She turned to Belinda with an exaggerated pout, her hands resting on her hips. "I think ZeZe's idea of a dinner party at Nohant is delightful, but must we really go in drag?"

Belinda observed with a hint of amusement, as she adjusted the collar of her own attire. She was clad in a simple yet elegant walking dress, a soft blue fabric that flowed gracefully to the floor. "Well, that's what you wanted, isn't it? To dress like a fashionable lady of society. Trust me, you'd be better off in something more understated like this," she remarked, motioning to her own dress with a knowing smile. Hazel scrutinized the flowing garment with its high neck and gently puffed sleeves, a hint of scepticism flickering across her face. "Honestly, it looks more like a nightgown than an outfit for socializing. But I'm really asking why the fuss about this dinner party? All this frippery seems a bit excessive."

"Have you not figured it out yet?" Belinda replied, a teasing tone to her voice. "Every extravagant detail is part of ZeZe's grand scheme to turn Nohant and the surrounding village into a flourishing tourist destination. This gathering is just the first of many to come, I suspect."

"Ah, I see," Hazel said, her brow furrowing thoughtfully as she practiced sitting down, carefully adjusting her skirt to accommodate the bustle.

The sharp sound of the charabanc horn pierced the crisp evening air, summoning the group from their respective Priory cells. They strolled with an air of anticipation toward the vehicle parked with its cover snugly in place against the coolness of the night. Andre and Walton shuffled awkwardly in their gentleman's attire, Walton's coat a cacophony of plaid patterns, while Andre opted for the sombre elegance of a black frock coat. ZeZe, Joan, and Jenny donned day dresses similar to Belinda's but in darker hues, each almost indistinguishable from the other. Gino, as expected, was dressed impeccably in a butler's uniform. When Hazel emerged from the Priory, her voluminous skirts billowing around her like a ship unfurling its sails, she sensed a ripple of suppressed laughter among her companions. She may be a galleon in full sail, but like that full-rigged sailing ship built principally for war, she was determined to take no prisoners.

As they awaited the last member of their party, the group settled into the charabanc, and Belinda was suddenly reminded of school outings filled with a thrill more potent than the events they had planned. Only the two Americans seemed genuinely engaged in the evening's whimsy. Walton, in an effort to adapt to the occasion, had affixed a pair of false sideburns to his cheeks. Nothing of this nature occurred in Nevada and Chicago or if it did they had clearly moved in the wrong circles.

Mrs Alice's appearance caused necks to crack as they turned to face the spectacle. Choosing to honour George Sand Mrs Alice portrayed the author in her male style dress, tailored black jacket and red trousers, trivial slippers ornamented with fringe. Her black wig parted in the middle, languid hair to her shoulders impartially framed her face. The consensus of the group was Mrs Alice had good intentions, but the style of garb, which was so elegant on Sand accentuating her femininity, in this case failed to hide the evidence of an aging overweight body on creaky legs, and skin the texture of beige crepe paper.

As the charabanc rolled through the gates of the Maison, the warm glow of candlelight flooded from the windows, casting dancing shadows across the courtyard and creating a magical scene against the backdrop of the darkening sky. A gaggle of villagers appeared near the entrance, their curious expressions betraying a rampant interest in the foreign guests. At a distance, near the Memorial Cross, a solitary figure observed quietly, blending into the night—a spectre named Obadiah, pondering what he might be missing by distancing himself from the festivities.

Upon entering the Salle à Manger, the guests were surrounded by the rich strains of a Chopin

Nocturne, masterfully played by a string quartet stationed in the Vestibule. The room, aglow with flickering candlelight that illuminated the silver plates and ancient glassware adorning the table, transported them to another era—one steeped in the artistic romance of Chopin and George Sand. As they stood awestruck, Gino appeared, offering each guest a shimmering glass of champagne with a practiced nod and a shady smile.

"A toast before you dine," Jenny announced casting an eye over the group, "we have a little surprise for you all. Rumour has it that there is a hidden secret within these walls that relates to our illustrious host, Chopin. Upon his passing, he insisted that his heart be interred in his native Poland, but whispers suggest that this burial was merely a deception—that the real heart may remain here in this very building."

Confused murmurs spread through the group, rippling like a wave. Andre's face reddened with indignation, ready to challenge the claims, but before he could utter a word, Jenny continued, her voice laced with simulated excitement. "I think you'll all enjoy this little adventure. Each of you will receive an envelope containing a map of the building, the specific room you are to search, and a clue. Perhaps you might even uncover the elusive heart!"

Gesturing dramatically, she signalled for Gino to distribute sealed envelopes bearing each guest's name. The group hesitated at first, bemused by the unexpected twist in their evening plans, but Joan, her spirit effervescent with enthusiasm, let out a joyous shriek and tore into her envelope. Her eyes lit up as she scrutinized the map, her laughter echoing through the room as she rushed towards the staircase leading to the upper level, her excitement infectious. Walton, momentarily startled and slightly embarrassed by his wife's fervour, managed a half-hearted smile as he scrambled to follow her. The remaining guests opened their envelopes, intrigued but cautious. They carefully unravelled the contents and began to formulate their own plans, slowly moving toward the designated area outlined in the maps. Andre, still aflame with frustration, desperately sought out Jenny, only to find that she was already out of sight, leaving only a stalwart Gino behind who, with a nonchalant shrug, offered no answers.

"What do you make of this new game?" Hazel mused aloud as she and Belinda examined their envelopes simultaneously.

"Well, for starters," Belinda huffed, shaken from her contemplative state, "they misspelled my name!" In the midst of the commotion, Walton rapidly came racing back down the stairs, breathless and wide-eyed, as he clutched his own map tightly. The evening, it seemed, was just beginning, and the allure of a hidden heart had ignited a fervour among them all. "Joan's in a blue room," he declared awkwardly, his voice tinged with excitement and a hint of nervousness. "Mine's down here," he added before lurching away in search of his own room, one sideburn flapping by his cheek.

Joan, filled with curiosity, tiptoed into what she now knew to be the Blue Boudoir. Her eyes widened in amazement at the opulence surrounding her, each element more luxurious than anything she had ever encountered back in Chicago, save perhaps for the grandeur of the Water Tower. The room was a breathtaking display of contrasting colours, where rich blue and crisp white adorned the walls and drapes, elegantly framing the tall windows. The baroque white lacquered armchairs seemed to beckon her to sit and linger a while. Tentatively, she stepped further into the chamber, her heart racing with anticipation. Nearby, a desk was cluttered with a scattering of open books, their pages yellowed with age. She caught sight of a note tucked among them. Snatching it up and glancing at the cryptic instructions provided to her, the clue read, 'O my Luve's like a red, red rose.' Her brow furrowed in confusion, as she scanned her surroundings for any signs of flowers. A bright red shiny object glinted from the corner of her eye, drawing her attention like a moth to a flame. It was a large, vibrant red heart, its surface smooth and inviting.

As they ascended the staircase to their assigned rooms, Belinda was headed for a Boudoir while Hazel strolled toward a nearby Ancienne Garde-Robe. Both were lost in thought, contemplating the clue that, in their case, had proven to be HEARTFELT. With only half-hearted enthusiasm, they began to search for their respective gifts. In the distance, the unmistakable sound of someone coughing reverberated through the halls. Harsh and violent.

"Someone doesn't seem to appreciate Chopin's music," Hazel remarked with a wry smile, trying to lighten the mood.

Belinda nodded, her face thoughtful. "Well, the cat's out of the bag when it comes to Chopin's heart—or rather, Andre's theory. I can't help but wonder, has Jenny known all along?" she speculated. The two began to ponder who could have conceived such an intricate party game...and why?

Abruptly, the distant music came to a halt, leaving a twitchy silence draping over the Maison. Standing at the doorway, Hazel's voice broke the stillness. "I think I've found my gift," she announced, holding aloft a heart-shaped potpourri bag, its label adorned with the emblem of a renowned perfumery, the fragrance wafting gently toward them. Belinda raised her own discovery triumphantly—a silk scarf exquisitely patterned with cascading red hearts. "And I found mine. All too easy," she chuckled, a hint of mischief in her eyes. "I wonder what treasures await Joan." Hazel glanced at her map, her brow furrowing in concentration. "Walton mentioned a blue room, so I assume that must be the Chambre Bleu, just down the hall."

The duo set off, pausing intermittently to peek into neighbouring rooms, admiring the intricate fittings and timeless furniture that enhanced each space with an air of antiquity.

Upon reaching the blue room, Belinda called out, "Joan? Have you discovered your gift?"

When silence answered her, they exchanged worried glances before stepping into the room. What they found stopped them in their tracks; Joan lay sprawled on the floor, an expression of shock frozen on her face. It was immediately clear that something was terribly wrong—her eyes were wide open, but her mouth was obstructed, choked with a mass of chocolate. Beside her was a half-empty, red heart-shaped box of chocolates, its lid askew. Next to that lay an envelope addressed elegantly to Mademoiselle ZeZe Dupont.

CHAPTER THIRTY-TWO

"Cyanide!" exclaimed Jenny, her voice laced with disbelief and fear. "Who would have had the audacity to do something so wicked?"

Hazel, with eyes sharp and unwavering, replied, "Well, for a start, the police seem to think *you* did." Her tone was matter of fact, as if stating the obvious to anyone who had been following the developments closely. A week had passed since the Maison—a once-idyllic setting now marred by tragedy—was declared a crime scene. The group had endured days of intense scrutiny, with Jenny being held by the authorities as the prime suspect in the shocking murder. The only reason for her eventual release had been the absence of her fingerprints on the chocolate box and a lack of any discernible motive for wanting ZeZe dead. Upon her return to the Priory, where the remaining members of the group stayed under police supervision, tension ran high. It was here, beneath the heavy atmosphere of suspicion and uncertainty, that Belinda and Hazel confronted her.

"I think it's time we finally lay everything bare," Belinda asserted, her expression resolute. "We need to make it known that ZeZe has been planning this tour as part of her schemes to transform Nohant into a bustling tourist haven, complete with all sorts of attractions, all while leveraging the legacies of George Sand, Chopin, and who knows who else."

Jenny's brow furrowed in disbelief. "You

know about that?"

"It didn't take long to piece it together," Belinda replied, casting a wary glance toward the driveway as a police car rolled into the garden, its siren fading into the background. "The crux of the matter is, did someone feel so strongly about ZeZe's plans that they were driven to murder her by poisoning her chocolates?"

Jenny wrung her hands, her anxiety palpable. "I understand how it looks," she said, her voice low. "But ZeZe had suggested giving the guests a small token, a keepsake from their visit to the Maison, something that would embody the experience if her plans came to fruition. I had prepared those gifts and placed a small rose brooch—a trivial trinket—intended for ZeZe to discover in the Blue Boudoir, to keep up the charade that she was merely one of the guests."

"Then how did the poisoned chocolates end up there?" said Hazel.

"I feel like I'm repeating what the police asked me," Jenny responded, a hint of frustration creeping into her voice. "But I genuinely don't know! Gino and I were following ZeZe's instructions. We placed the gifts in each room and prepared the envelopes just as she directed."

"But Joan got ZeZe's envelope," Belinda reminded her, urgency rising in her tone.

"That's correct," Jenny admitted, her expression mixing regret and confusion. "Gino must have mixed them up. Joan was so excited to receive what she thought was a prize that she didn't take the moment to check the envelope—she just tore it open and hurried to the Blue Room."

"Where the poisoned chocolates were laid out, instead of your inexpensive rose brooch," Hazel concluded, her mind racing through the implications. "Assuming your version of events is accurate," she continued, "and you and Gino were acting on ZeZe's orders, it means anyone in the group could potentially be the murderer."

Belinda interjected, "Except they would have needed prior knowledge of how the gifts were distributed."

"That's just it," Jenny said, her voice tinged with despair. "Only ZeZe and I were in the know."

"And Gino," Belinda added, emphasizing his role in the unfolding mystery.

At that moment, a disturbance from the garden captured their attention. They turned to see Walton, accompanied by the police, loading his luggage into their vehicle. "Is he being arrested?" Belinda asked, a flash of hope rising within her. Jenny shook her head, her expression grave.

"No. They've released Joan's body, and he's taking her back home to Chicago for her parents to bury her."

"So he's free to go?" Belinda queried, disbelief etched on her face.

"He has to report to the local police, though. Just in case there are any further developments concerning Joan's murder," Jenny clarified, suggesting a strange mix of sympathy and suspicion toward Walton. As the police car reversed and pulled away, carrying Walton on what had to be a sorrowful journey, Hazel spoke up. "So let's assume he didn't stand to inherit a fortune and actually had genuine feelings for that, well, whiny voice of Joan's. If that's the case, he had no motive to harm her, which means we're left with seven suspects still capable of murder—counting both Bel and me." The tension in the air thickened, and the three women were each acutely aware of the ever-tightening knot of danger that surrounded them.

CHAPTER THIRTY-THREE

The chill of the night air bit at Obadiah's skin as he stepped out from the cramped confines of his rented room in the Nohant cottage. The once-inviting space was now beginning to feel like a cell, imprisoning him in his solitude and unrelenting thoughts. He knew he could no longer avoid the looming confrontation with the tour group; he would have to humble himself, seek their understanding, and perhaps find solace among them. An unsettling weight pressed on his chest, yet he found himself hesitating, caught in a web of uncertainty. He opted for his nightly refuge, the familiar path leading him toward the welcoming shadowy embrace of the Church of Saint-Anne. The ancient, sacred aura radiating from the imposing structure offered him a flicker of comfort against the relentless tide of self-doubt washing over him. It was a temporary balm, but it helped restore a sense of freedom he longed for. Obadiah's reluctance was rooted in a recent incident. The group had once again found themselves embroiled in a murder mystery, leading to lengthy interrogations with the police that had cast a dark cloud over their travels. He had heard whispers of suspicion from his landlady, a fountain of malice, who claimed, with a dramatic flourish and the crossing of her heart, that they were all murderers. The villagers, it seemed, had been gripped by fear, securing their doors and windows tight against the perceived threat that had descended upon their quiet community.

As he lingered in the shadows, soft voices carried through the cool evening air, drawing his thoughts back to the present. He instinctively pressed himself further into the cloak of darkness as he spied Andre and a woman he recognized as Marie—a local villager, whose rustic beauty had earned her the nickname "nymph du prairie" from his landlady. The old woman had uttered the title with a mix of envy and disdain, as if wishing to distance herself from any sins associated with the village whispers.

Marie approached the gates to the Maison, her movements graceful as she unlocked the barrier and handed the keys to Andre. With a quick goodbye, she melted away into the velvety night, leaving the heavy silence to settle over the grounds once more. Andre, illuminating the path with a beam of light, pushed open the front door and stepped into the building, oblivious to Obadiah's hidden presence. Curiosity ignited within the observer, overpowering any remnants of fear or hesitation. Padding softly on the flagstones, Obadiah followed the direction of Andre's light with a burgeoning thrill. The moon, playing its part in this midnight escapade, parted the clouds overhead, casting a glow that guided him along the path toward the sinister Maison. A shroud of mist curled around him, suggesting secrets of the long-lost souls connected to this place. He shivered involuntarily, quickening his pace until he finally slipped into the Vestibule. Ahead, he could see

Andre's flashlight darting upwards, up the curved staircase that climbed to the Chambre Bleu.

A curious force tugged at Andre, tempting him with the promise of discovery. As he stepped into the room, his heart raced with anticipation, a tremor of excitement coursing through him. The air inside was thick with the scent of musty perfume and past times. Had he, perhaps, stumbled upon the hidden sanctum of Chopin's heart?

Below him, the gloom enveloped Obadiah as he navigated the unlit room, faint glimmers of moonlight filtering in through the windows only heightening the foreboding atmosphere. He strained to listen for any sound, any indication of where Andre had ventured. A distant noise broke the stillness. "Andre?" he called out softly, though he suppressed his voice, uncertain if he truly wished to be heard. Recalling the staircase from his earlier visit, he sensed rather than knew where to go, instinctively positioning himself towards the right side of the entrance. He paused, his foot finding the first step, anticipation making him hold his breath and dread coiling in his stomach. Feeling with trembling fingers for the banister, he ascended one step at a time.

Dust particles danced in the beam of Andre's flashlight, swirling in the dimness as the latter swung the light, searching for any clue—anything that would lead him to the heart he sought. The mounted portraits lining the walls seemed to survey the intruder with expressions that vacillated between sorrow and indifference. Among them, George Sand's image loomed predominate, her distrustful gaze pinning him in place as if questioning his very presence.

Reaching the top floor, Obadiah found his heart pounding. Noises and the occasional flicker of Andre's flashlight indicated the source of the activity ahead, drawing him closer despite the gnawing fear that enveloped him. He inched toward the doorway, heart racing, every fibre of his being alert to the danger of discovery. Peering tentatively into the room, he caught sight of Andre—a shadowy figure illuminated by the beam, hunched earnestly over a desk as he rifled through the drawers in a frantic search. Andre muttered a curse. a wave of frustration spilling from his lips as he grappled with the realization that the heart could not possibly be found as easily as he had hoped. The Chambre Bleu had been his logical first choice; after all, it had once served as George Sand's boudoir, and it stood to reason that she would have kept her beloved Chopin's heart close. Yet, that assumption was fraught with complications. After all, George had conducted numerous affairs with a string of literary luminaries and artistic figures—the author of 'Carmen', a dramatist, an actor, fellow writers, and radicals. Had she truly preserved the hearts of them all? The thought sent a chill creeping down his spine, compelling him to banish the horrific imagery from his mind.

Shaking off the disquieting thoughts,

Andre returned his focus to the search, frustration turning into panic. He swung the flashlight across the opulent room, suddenly freezing as the beam revealed a startling sight: a reflection hovering just behind him in the mirror—a ghostly apparition. Andre jolted around, focusing his light on the spectre.

"Obadiah!" Andre's voice blared, an enraged accusation carving through the silence as he charged toward him. Obadiah's heart momentarily stopped, but the primal instinct to flee overcame his paralysis. He darted into the enveloping shadows, abandoning any semblance of caution. His feet raced to the staircase, propelled by fear of the confrontation more than the worry of tumbling into the pitch-black abyss below. He reached the landing and skidded to a halt.

In the pitch black he sensed an even darker image. A violent punch in his back sent him reeling into the void and tumble after tumble, the steps struck blow after blow. As he was just about to hit the last step, before his head cracked on stone, he realised there had been someone else in the building.

CHAPTER THIRTY-FOUR

"He's coming round." The voice reverberated through a fog of disorientation, distant and ethereal, as Obadiah blinked heavily and gradually peeled his eyelids apart. The world slowly materialized out of the haze of sterile white, revealing two shapes looming above him. They were indistinct at first, and no matter how hard he tried, he couldn't bring them into sharp relief. In a state of confusion, he instinctively reached for his wire-rimmed spectacles—the ones that habitually perched on the bridge of his nose—but found nothing there. His hand grazed over what felt like a cloche hat resting awkwardly on his head, its fabric strange and unfamiliar, and an all-consuming headache pulsated through his temples, sharp and insistent. Panic rose within him like a wave as he realized that his arm was tangled in a curious arrangement of transparent tubes snaking out from his skin. Desperately glancing upwards, he could just make out a bag suspended above him, the tubes stretching taut and draining a clear liquid into his body like lifelines from some unknown source. A question clawed at his throat as he struggled to cry out, but only the croak of a dry voice escaped his lips. "What...is that?"

"Gin," replied a voice with a hint of playful sarcasm. "I tried to get one but sécurité sociale told me to naff off." The words came from a woman with a strikingly fierce aura—Hazel, he vaguely remembered. Surprisingly, this unexpected response did little to soothe Obadiah's qualms, and he inwardly sighed; he had always preferred a Cherry Bounce to gin.

"What is this place? Where am I?" he managed to croak, his voice barely above a whisper. Another creature, this one with an air of calm authority, spoke next. "You're in the hospital, Obadiah," said Belinda, her Australian accent cutting through the disorientation, "you had a fall and hit your head rather badly."

Obadiah instinctively raised a cautious hand to his head, fingers brushing against a bulk of the bandages swaddling it. "Oh?" His voice held a mixture of disbelief and concern.

"You've fractured your skull," Belinda explained, her tone balanced between clinical and compassionate. "It's a linear fracture, thankfully, so no operation is necessary. They're managing your pain and keeping you here for observation."

With great effort, Obadiah squeezed his eyes shut tightly then open, willing them to clear. In the dim light, the shapes before him began to solidify: the Australian woman with her determined gaze and the English woman with an expression of restrained sympathy. Embarrassment flushed his cheeks as the full weight of his predicament crashed down upon him. There was no escaping the conversation he had dreaded. He rifled desperately through his foggy mind for the carefully crafted lies he had rehearsed a million times in anticipation of this moment. Before he could gather enough courage to speak, the English woman intersected his thoughts. "What were you doing in the Maison?"

"The Maison?" he echoed, confusion still reigning.

"Don't prevaricate," Hazel pressed, a stern edge infused in her voice. "I mean the Maison de George Sand. You were found there apparently after falling down the stairs."

As the cerebral mist enveloping Obadiah's mind began to lift, flashes of fragmented memories burst forth like lightning bolts. The night—the fall—the indescribable sensation of plummeting into darkness. "The pole..." he muttered, his voice trailing off into a whisper. Belinda and Hazel exchanged glances, concern mingled with uncertainty. Had he suffered irreversible brain damage? "The Polish fellow," Obadiah continued, the strength returning to his voice as fragments of memory coalesced.

"Andre?" "What about him?" Belinda pressed, her interest sharpening.

"I followed him. It was nighttime, pitch black. But a woman gave him keys. He went inside and I followed." Panic began to creep into his voice, pulling him back to fragmented fears.

"What woman?" Hazel demanded.

Obadiah hesitated, at first instinctively shaking his head, but then reconsidered. "A villager... I think her name was Marie. He went upstairs into a room and began searching it. When he saw me watching, he turned on me, and I panicked and ran to the stairs. It was utterly black, and I fell." The recollection felt increasingly vivid, though still shrouded in shadow.

"You were unconscious and not found until the next morning," Belinda interjected, "But if Andre was there, he could have gone for help."

"Can you remember if Andre found anything? And what room was he searching?" Hazel's inquiries were rapid; each one layered with urgency. Obadiah frowned, frustration boiling beneath the surface. What was the room again? It had been so dark; the details felt elusive. "He was still searching when he came to confront me, so I don't think he discovered anything. The room had blue fittings and was really ornate."

"The Chambre Bleu," Hazel murmured, a spark of recognition igniting.

"Where Joan was murdered," Belinda muttered under her breath, her expression turning grave. She cast a profound, lingering look at Obadiah. "We'll let you rest now and visit tomorrow."

As both women rose to leave, their footsteps echoing softly in the sterile ambiance, Obadiah extended a hand weakly. "Wait. There's something else I remember," he said, urgency thickening his tone. "On the staircase. In the dark. Someone pushed me down."

CHAPTER THIRTY-FIVE

ZeZe stood at her window in the Priory, the atmosphere surrounding her reminiscent of a grand theatre balcony, where she could play the role of an observer, taking in an unfolding drama in the courtyard below. In her line of sight, the garden area became a stage set for two figures—the young Australian woman and the English woman both seated comfortably, yet visibly tense. What did the English call them? Coffee sisters? Gossip over coffee? In their case, Sœurs apéritives.

They sipped on their afternoon tipple, their drinks clinking quietly as they engaged in a hushed conversation, punctuated by nervous glances over their shoulders as though fearing a hidden menace.

The tranquillity of their gathering was abruptly pierced when a police car rolled into the courtyard, its sirens stilled but the ominous presence unmistakable. A figure emerged from the vehicle—Obadiah. His eyes scanned the scene, a predatory look, before locking onto the women.. It was then that ZeZe noted the tension elevate; the strange, plump American who had mysteriously vacated the tour was now back, and his return rippled with implications. Obadiah started speaking to the women, his tone low and conveyed a sense of urgency.

Abruptly, the scene shifted even more dramatically. The trio at the garden table, initially lost in their discussion, turned in collective astonishment as they witnessed Andre being escorted out from the hotel by police officers. His expression was a mixture of shock and bewilderment as he was guided towards the awaiting patrol car.

Almost immediately, a taxi punctured the thick air of tension, rolling noisily into the grounds. ZeZe was taken aback when Macca emerged from the vehicle. His eyes, initially reflecting curiosity, quickly locked onto the unfolding commotion, searching for context. The group's attention was centred on the departing police car.

Paying the driver Macca stepped onto the cobblestones. His eyes found ZeZe's, who was still frozen at her window, her breath held in anticipation. Without delay, he hastened over to join the trio, an unexpected return that stirred ZeZe's curiosity further. She still sought some video material for her project, but the budding rapport between Macca and Belinda took her by surprise; even from a distance, the spark of connection was palpable.

Obadiah was recounting his recent adventure to Macca, his tone now brimming with a lively enthusiasm that contrasted sharply with his previous demeanour. His recent brushes with French police—having undergone fingerprinting, providing a DNA swab, not to mention the frisson of being interrogated by French Police investigating a murder, which made his brush with the County Sheriff in North Carolina pale insignificantly...it was only a minor incident and the cat recovered...so the reluctance and inhibition he had initially shown was replaced by loquaciousness, enthusiasm, and vitality which amused Macca who was meeting the American for the first time.

"I was a stranger living in the village during the time of the murders," Obadiah exclaimed animatedly, recounting his experiences with wide-eyed wonder.

"And who are you?" Macca asked, taking a seat near Belinda, his curiosity genuine.

"This is Obadiah; he's part of the tour group. Long story. I'll tell you later," Belinda chimed in quickly, her tone hinting at layered histories among them. Turning her attention back to Obadiah, she probed, "So, what's your interest in Chopin's heart?"

Obadiah looked perplexed, puzzled by her question. "Chopin? No, I'm interested in Uncle Henry."

At that, Belinda and the others glanced at each other in unison, all temporarily baffled. "Uncle Henry who?" she inquired, intrigued.

"Henry James," Obadiah replied matter-of-factly, as if it were common knowledge. "He and Edith Wharton visited Nohant on their Motor Flight. We're duplicating it with this tour."

"Good grief," Hazel interjected, the realization settling in slowly. "I'd almost forgotten that; two murders tend to cloud the issue somewhat, don't they?"

"So, Henry James, the writer, is your uncle?" Macca asked, his voice laced with doubt. Obadiah glanced at him, a slight shrug escaping him. "Well, I call him uncle. The thing is, I think I'm related to an American friend of his—or more so, to his family really, but I have no proof."

"So you're doing the tour as a tribute to him?" Belinda ventured again, gauging his seriousness.

"Oh, it's more than that," Obadiah said earnestly, his eyes lighting up with excitement. "I intend to ask him."

Three pairs of eyes exchanged incredulous glances, the atmosphere thick with comic disbelief. Macca cleared his throat, a bemused smile creeping onto his face. "Umm...you may not remember, but Henry James died sometime in the early part of the twentieth century, or thereabouts." His tone turned condescending as he added, "How do you intend asking him?"

Obadiah remained undeterred, his expression earnest yet slightly puzzled. "Well... I talk to dead people."

In the inebriated silence that followed, from the corner of her eye, Belinda saw Hazel's hand creep inevitably towards the gin and tonic.

CHAPTER THIRTY-SIX

Andre, enveloped in a heavy veil of Gallic silence, sat uncomfortably in the back seat of the police car as it wound its way toward Châteauroux. A knot of apprehension twisted in his stomach as he anticipated the second interrogation looming ahead. He sensed that the gendarmes were hoping for him to unwittingly let something slip—an inconsistency, perhaps, or a clue that could lead to his condemnation. Despite their intentions, Andre was resolute; he had no additional information to disclose. His thoughts, however, were firmly anchored in the unsettling image of that portly American, Obadiah, who had seemingly returned to the fold in company with the police. The prospect of Obadiah revealing his observations during the botched break-in attempt at the Maison gnawed at Andre's mind, especially since the incident had left him with a cut on his hand. Not to mention, Obadiah had witnessed him combing through the Blue Room—the murder room—looking for clues. Was this the motive behind his pending interrogation? Andre could not fathom what plausible explanation he could offer. He had no desire to divulge his quest for Chopin's heart—a secret he meant to safeguard until he could unmask the convoluted deception at play and reap not only academic acclaim but also significant financial rewards. As the car rattled down the narrow, winding roads, he knew he had to craft a convincing cover story. Searching for clues to the identity of the murderer? Presenting himself as an amateur detective might just do the trick. With that thought in mind, he mentally slipped into a Poirot-esque mode, reassuring himself that this persona would suffice for the impending interview. If only he had a fine moustache as a nod to the famous sleuth, but without a war injury to conceal, he felt at a disadvantage.

CHAPTER THIRTY-SEVEN

"This is Frankie!" exclaimed Obadiah, as if introducing an old friend to the group gathered around him. Belinda, Hazel, and Macca exchanged glances, their curiosity piqued. "It's a cell phone—a mobile phone," declared Belinda. The gadget in Obadiah's hand bore similarities to contemporary technology; however, upon closer inspection, the trio noticed an antenna, a diminutive screen, and an array of buttons that hinted at something more unusual.

"I saw it in your suitcase," Belinda added, a hint of accusation creeping into her tone. Obadiah frowned, his expression a mix of surprise and irritation. "You went through my luggage?"

"On that day you ditched the tour in Amiens. I was searching for you and noticed your case was open." The explanation seemed to pacify Obadiah, who redirected his attention to the sombre landscape of the Nohant cemetery. The fading light, cast an almost ghostly aura over the resting place, which guarded the many members of the Sand family from the tribulations of earthly suffering. Dominating the others was the imposing tomb dedicated to George Sand, her name boldly etched into the stone. Below it lay a pristine white rose, recently left as a tribute by an unknown admirer.

"So," Macca said, breaking the momentary silence, "what exactly does 'Frankie' do?"

Obadiah's face lit up with a smirk, relishing

the opportunity to educate the uninformed. "It's a Spook Box. I named it Frankie after its inventor."

The mention of 'spook' sent a ripple of apprehension through Hazel, prompting her to glance warily around in the quickly darkening twilight. A small speaker device was affixed to the Spook Box, and Obadiah seemed eager to impress his small audience with its capabilities. "Spook boxes are controversial among ghost hunters— some supporters and many sceptics. The idea is that spirits can harness energy from the Spook Box as it cycles through various channels or radio frequencies, generating words and, on occasion, complete sentences from the departed."

Hazel let out a deep sigh, accumulating her disdain for the macabre entertainment before her. "I've been to some wild parties and heard some crazy shall we say —merde, out of respect for George, our French hostess, who is trapped as she is in her tomb. She has to listen to this nonsense. I don't." With that, she turned on her heel, tripping over a headless stone cherub, and made her way out of the cemetery toward the waiting Citroën, craving comfort in the encroaching darkness.

"I've heard of this," Macca said, casting a dubious glance at Obadiah. "And it really works?"

"The proof of the pudding is in the eating. To quote Uncle Henry, 'Our doubt is our passion, and our passion is our task'," Obadiah replied, flicking several switches on the device. As he twisted a dial, the night air became charged with erratic static bursting from the speaker. The sound fluctuated, faded into near silence, then suddenly surged back, dominating the atmosphere like a ghostly presence. Belinda felt a shiver race down her spine, the eerie ambiance growing more pronounced as the static danced across the small screen.

"What happens now?" Macca inquired, his interest piqued despite himself.

"I scan the graves and ask if anyone is present," Obadiah proclaimed confidently, making a slow sweep of the cemetery with the Spook Box, moving meticulously from left to right and then back again.

Belinda started to question the sanity of their endeavour, contemplating whether Hazel had indeed made the right choice by abandoning the folly. "We know the Sand family is here, but do we—"

"Shhh," Obadiah interrupted sharply, licking his lips in anticipation as he peered intently into the creeping shadows. "Is anybody there?" An oppressive silence hung in the air, broken only by the relentless static that rose and fell in volume. "My name is Obadiah James," he declared, even the introduction eliciting no answer from the unseen realm.

Belinda coughed lightly, not being able to hold back, and then suggested, "I think you might get a better response if you spoke in French."

"Oh!" Obadiah exclaimed, his eyes brightening with realization. "I translated my questions into French." He began to rummage through his pockets, finally extracting a crumpled piece of paper. "But—oh no! I can't read it in the dark!"

"No worries," said Macca and produced a pocket torch. Obadiah hurriedly found the beam of light and peered at the paper. "Jay my apple Obadiah James."

Belinda and Macca both gave a snort of amusement which they hurriedly converted into a cough and clearing their throats. Undeterred, Obadiah continued. "Yatal quell qoon là-bass?" The muffled sniggers of his companions was echoed by a night bird's cry on finding a thorn in its nest.

"I think after all," said Belinda, "it's probably best to stay with English. I'm sure they were knowledgeable and can understand it."

Resolutely, Obadiah continued. "Is anyone there?" He scanned the site with the Box. Amidst the static,

*** *qui***

Obadiah gave a small jump for joy. "Yes! I mean, Wee!"

The sudden faint vocal response took Macca and Belinda and by surprise. She felt the hairs on her neck rise. But the excitement faded when the static continued alone, teasing with undulating promise emitting an occasional burp or fragment of word.

"We mean you no harm," said Obadiah, "what is your name?" As the minutes ticked by the spirits were either playing hard to get, thought Belinda, or else trying to translate the English request into nineteenth century French.

A few more sweeps of the cemetery with the Box and Obadiah said, "I need to speak to my Uncle Henry. Henry James. Is he here?" Fighting through the static, a flat metallic voice.

Edith

Hazel huddled against the evening chill, her breath visible in the crisp air as she settled deeper into the worn passenger seat of the old car. She had long since given up any hope that the vehicle's minimalistic interior would boast any sort of heating feature, relying instead on her thick coat and soft scarf to ward off the biting cold. As she waited for Belinda, Macca, and the ever-exuberant Obadiah to wrap up their lengthy discussion about spirits and spectres, she couldn't help but feel a pang of unease—especially regarding Obadiah's erratic behaviour, which had begun to feel increasingly unpredictable. To distract herself from the boredom of the situation, she replayed flashes of the evening's events in her mind, each one tinged with a sense of foreboding.

Andre's unexpected summons to the police station lingered at the forefront of her thoughts. What had compelled the action by the police? Obadiah's sudden reemergence into the group only added further layers to the tangled web of mysteries surrounding them all. It struck her as odd how his supposed connection to the infamous Henry James intertwined with Andre's determined quest for Chopin's heart. Then there was ZeZe and her ambitious scheme to turn the quaint village of Nohant into a commercial hub for tourists. And Mrs. Alice—her film project loomed, stirring questions about whether Obadiah's pursuits would somehow serve her cinematic aspirations. So many threads, spinning and twisting, and yet the picture remained murky. A chilling breeze swept through the night as the final hints of twilight faded away, enveloping Hazel in darkness.

A sudden flicker of movement caught her eye—an orb of light gliding towards the Maison gate, faint yet distinct against the canvas of night. It was as if the clouds decided to momentarily take part in the mystery—moonbeams illuminated ZeZe's silhouette as she made her way, torch in hand, into the grounds of the old estate. The ethereal glow vanished almost immediately, leaving Hazel in deepening shadows, her mind racing. What on earth was ZeZe doing at the Maison at such a late hour? Before she could delve deeper into her thoughts, the sound of footsteps broke the silence nearby. Could it be the others returning from their supernatural discussions? Just as she began to feel a comfort in the thought, a ghostly figure brushed past the car door and headed toward the gates. A flash of light from a mobile phone revealed Gino's familiar face—clearly he was engaged in a call. ZeZe and Gino together at this hour? Hazel's curiosity was spurred further; she recalled Belinda's tale of seeing ZeZe and Gino together, which lent a certain air of secrecy to their rendezvous. But what had drawn them to the Maison at this hour?

Curiosity may have killed the cat, Hazel mused, but she was willing to risk it. With a silent resolve, she maneuverer herself out of the car, carefully ensuring her movements wouldn't betray her. The pitch-black night was daunting, but a swift click on her phone activated the torchlight, casting a weak yet guiding glow that helped her navigate the uneven path to the front door. To her surprise, as she stepped across the threshold, the interior lights flickered on, presenting a warm beacon against the oppressive darkness outside. Her nerves heightened in anticipation, she cautiously ventured into the Vestibule, heart pounding with both adrenaline and apprehension.

To her left, she caught snippets of hushed whispers, their tones conspiratorial. Adjusting her approach, she edged closer, her curiosity propelling her forward. What she stumbled upon surprised her—a small theatre with a quaint stage and proscenium, perfectly preserved yet possessing an air of neglect. The whispers grew clearer now, revealing just enough to pique her interest. A doorway stood ajar, leading to an adjacent room. Hazel crept towards it and peered around the doorframe. Inside, ZeZe and Gino were huddled together, their heads bent over a curious assortment of small marionette dolls, intricately crafted with delicate features that seemed to spring to life under the muted lighting from above. As if sensing her presence, they turned sharply, their gazes landing on Hazel with a mixture of surprise and recognition.

Discovered, it was futile for her to retreat, so she straightened her posture and feigned nonchalance. "Couldn't sleep, so I took a stroll," Hazel stated, an impish grin on her lips. "I saw the light on and the door open, so I thought I'd just wander in." Yet, the bemused expressions on her companions' faces told her they weren't buying her ploy for a second. Trying to mask her unease, she picked up one of the marionettes, its wooden body surprisingly light in her hands. "What quaint little toys," she observed with feigned innocence. "I gave up playing with dolls when I was five." Her gaze shifted to ZeZe, a sly smile creeping across her face. "But some people never quite leave the nursery—often referred to as the Peter Pan Syndrome, don't you think?" Her teasing tone lingered in the air, a mischievous jab not meant to lighten the unexpected tension of the moment.

CHAPTER THIRTY-NINE

"So, fundamentally, it's just white noise, and you're saying that spirits can use it to communicate? Is that the gist of it?" Macca asked, his voice tinged with scepticism as he leaned back in his chair, cradling a dwindling glass of whiskey. The group had gathered in the cozy Priory lounge for a nightcap, the dimly lit room echoing with the warmth of flickering candlelight. Hazel, nestled in the corner with a drink in hand, savoured the restorative properties of her gin and tonic. The evening's discussions had taken a ghostly turn, and while she found Belinda's tales of phantom voices unsettling, she was unwilling to lay bare her anxiety. "Rubbish! Like I said before, it's all just a joke," she retorted with affected indifference, masking her unease with bravado.

"You didn't actually hear the voice, though," Belinda replied, her tone still laced with disbelief. She was grappling with the haunting sound she had encountered, the experience unexpectedly lingering.

Obadiah, sipping his drink thoughtfully, interjected, "As you say, Macca. The theory is that spirits use that ambient noise to initiate contact and communicate with the living. As they're thought to be composed of energy, enabling this interaction."

Hazel shook her head dismissively. "I think 'composed of' is a stretch here," she countered, a slight edge of concern creeping into her voice. "Otherwise, who knows what might come through?

It could be a malicious demon wreaking havoc on anyone foolish enough to summon it."

A smirk flickered across Belinda's lips. "Hazel, you've just inadvertently revealed that you think there's a grain of truth in what we're saying. You're giving the game away." Frustrated by her unintentional slip—her internal alarm at the thought of the Spook Box being real painted across her face—Hazel took refuge in her drink. A reflective silence enveloped the group; each member lost in their own thoughts about the evening's bizarre events.

Sensing the need to break the tension and dispel any lingering fears, Hazel sat up straight, her posture resolute. "While you all were occupied in the graveyard, I found my own adventure in the Maison," she declared, her eyes gleaming with self-satisfaction as the others turned to her in surprise.

"How did you manage to get in?" Belinda asked, curiosity piquing in her voice.

"Well," Hazel replied eagerly , "I followed ZeZe and Gino. They slipped into a room off the entrance hall which I think is called the theatre, and guess what? They were playing with dolls."

Belinda's frown deepened. "Dolls?" she echoed.

"Yes, not your typical dolls, though," Hazel explained, relishing the intrigue she was creating. "These were all kinds of shapes and sizes, dressed in various theatrical costumes, like actors preparing for a grand performance."

"Puppets?" Macca interjected, eyebrows raised in interest.

"Marionettes," Belinda corrected him with a hint of excitement. "I recall reading about those in our tour brochure. Something about—"

Before she could finish her thought, the distinct sound of the front door opening interrupted them. Heads turned in unison as Andre stepped into the foyer, his expression grim and his posture rigid. He glanced momentarily at the gathered group, hesitated as if weighing his next move, but then continued on silently towards his room.

"I'd pay good money to know why the police wanted to speak to him again," Hazel remarked, as a glimmer of curiosity ignited in her mind, her thoughts racing through possibilities.

Upstairs, Andre approached his room, the weight of the evening heavy on his shoulders. Just as he reached for his doorknob, another door swung open. He paused, startled, and turned to see ZeZe standing there, framed in the doorway as if she were a mysterious apparition herself. "I think we need to talk," she said, her tone grave and serious, suggesting that whatever conversation lay ahead wouldn't be trivial.

CHAPTER FORTY

Mrs. Alice carefully lowered her video camera, the weight of its significance resting heavily in her hands. Following the tragic death of her brother, Henry, the responsibility of researching and producing their long-cherished film dream now fell solely to her. It was a monumental undertaking to envision and realize such a project single-handedly; Henry had always been her trusted partner in navigating the complexities of creative production. Yet, she felt a flicker of determination ignite within her—she possessed the strength and resolve to carry on, bolstered by the tantalizing prospect of an enormous financial return that awaited this endeavour. They had envisaged a grand cinematic adventure, a spectacular epic chronicling the motor travels of literary legends Edith Wharton and Henry James, while daring to explore the intimacies and hidden romances of their private lives. As if that weren't enough, she also aspired to interweave the lives of George Sand and Chopin through vivid flashback scenes, transforming the narrative into a lavish retelling of artistic genius both literary and musical. To sweeten the pot, she envisioned infusing the story with a sprinkle of salacious Hollywood flair, highlighting the more risqué elements of this monumental film, designed to entice audiences and provoke discussion. To elevate the project's profile, she planned to cast top-name stars alongside the hottest director in the industry, believing this would generate significant public interest. Moreover, if she could concoct a marital spat between her leading actors, she would be gifted free publicity, drawing throngs of moviegoers to cinemas around the globe. With steely resolve, she raised her camera once more, intent on capturing the essence of the Blue Boudoir around her. The art department would painstakingly need to recreate Maison Nohant within a studio, and she was adamant that every detail be meticulously accurate—down to the last ornament. This would serve not only as authenticity but also an enticing hook for promotional purposes. As she panned the camera over the grand, antique bed, another thought suddenly pierced her mind. This wasn't just any room; it was infamously known as the murder room. Here, a tragic incident had taken place—a young woman from Chicago had been poisoned by chocolates, which had been intended for someone else, someone named ZeZe. Could this unsettling history serve as the seed of inspiration for a murder mystery film set in such an environment? She tucked this idea away for future consideration with a sense of intrigue.

Eager to continue her exploration, Mrs. Alice descended the curved staircase that led to the ground level. With her camera firmly in hand, she wandered into what the guidebook had declared was the Theatre. It was in this very room that George Sand had first tested her plays before a welcoming audience of friends, all before they graced the professional stages of Paris. Yet,

Mrs. Alice found little excitement in the rather nondescript space. Still, she dutifully recorded the stage area, knowing it would serve as a reference in her ever-evolving vision. As she turned to inspect a small room connected to the Theatre, a spark of curiosity ignited within her; perhaps it would hold some hidden promise. With the camera rolling, she aimed it as she stepped inside. The room was cozy, almost cramped, but on the table at its centre lay an assortment of dolls, each one dressed in elaborate costumes representing various historical periods. She moved closer, intent on capturing the intricate details of these curious figurines with her camera when a sudden noise behind her sent a jolt of fear through her. She swung the camera around, the lens capturing a dark shape that darted across her field of vision. Before she could comprehend what was happening, a swift, shadowy movement sent a sharp blow crashing against her head. In an instant, the world faded to black as Mrs. Alice crumpled to the floor in a heap, her camera still recording, oblivious to the unfolding chaos as it documented the scene.

CHAPTER FORTY-ONE

With a sparkle of determination in her eye, Hazel formulated a plan to unearth the mysteries shrouding Andre's past. She believed that the key to gaining his trust lay in a delicate dance of seduction. As she spotted him immersed in his work in the Priory courtyard, his brows furrowed in concentration over his laptop, she decided to cast an enchanting spell over the encounter. With a subtle adjustment of her demeanour, she intended to steer the conversation toward his origins and experiences, all the while hoping to lower his defences and coax out the secrets surrounding Frédéric Chopin's heart.

"I see you're a slave to the computer," she declared boldly as she settled into the seat opposite him. As she did, she caught Andre's attention, his initial glance a mix of irritation and tentative approval. "It seems we haven't had the chance to really connect since that altogether delightful drink in Beauvais," she teased, intentionally crossing her legs to let the hem of her skirt slide up, revealing more of her thigh.

Andre grinned at her obvious ploy, momentarily thankful for the distraction from his screen. "True, I seem to have neglected my social life," he replied, his tone laced with a hint of regret. "You must admit that time for leisurely social interactions has been a scarce resource lately."

Hazel nodded in understanding. She couldn't

argue with his reasoning. "Are the local gendarmes giving you trouble, then?" she prodded, curious about the apprehension she sensed beneath his composed exterior. Andre's expression darkened slightly. "Oh, merely a misunderstanding," he dismissed, waving a hand as if to brush off the matter entirely. Although Hazel wasn't entirely convinced by his nonchalance, she realized that pressing further in this line of questioning would likely be futile for the moment. "So, what are your thoughts on George Sand?" she pivoted, eager to delve deeper into their discussion.

"Without a doubt, she was a remarkable French writer. So remarkable, in fact, there was a recent proposal to inter her in the Panthéon alongside Victor Hugo and Émile Zola. That proposal was, however, rejected, leaving her here in Nohant," Andre said, his voice tinged with both admiration and frustration.

"When we last spoke, you mentioned you hoped to uncover something of value to Poland while here in Nohant, presumably regarding Chopin?" Hazel pressed, keen to delve into the layers of mystery encasing the man before her.

He leaned back, fingers steepling as he mulled over her words. " You no doubt allude to the statement made the night of the murder, that Chopin's heart was hidden in the Maison. He was buried in Père-Lachaise Cemetery in Paris, as you're well aware. We visited his tomb together. However, word has it that his heart was sent to Warsaw after his death. During World War II, the Nazis not only banned his music but also made off with the heart."

"That must have deeply unsettled the Polish people, I imagine?" Hazel spoke, feeling the weight of the historical disaster.

"Undoubtedly," Andre replied, his tone grave. "But post-war, it was reinterred in the church, where it remained undisturbed until recently. A group of researchers examined it in secret to ensure its container was still intact and undamaged, as any compromise could lead to the heart's deterioration."

Hazel swatted away an irritating fly and shielded her eyes from the bright sun overhead. "But how do we know for certain it is Chopin's heart? And who relocated it to Poland in the first place?"

"In the days following his death, his sister, Ludwika, cleverly smuggled it from Paris to Warsaw in a jar of cognac. The jar, coupled with the liquid, protected it for nearly two centuries," he explained, his voice imbued with reverence for the tale.

"But it could just as easily belong to anyone, couldn't it?" Hazel said, teasingly raising an eyebrow at him.

Andre shot her a side-eye filled with playful reproach. "Ludwika was with Chopin in his final days; she took great care of him, especially towards the end. The heart was kept in her residence in Warsaw."

"Talk about morbid," Hazel remarked with a hint of mischief. "Keeping your brother's heart in a pickle jar?"

Ignoring her jibe, Andre continued, "Eventually, it moved to the Church of St. Krzyża, where it remained hidden away in the crypt, forgotten by all. Years later, a search led to its recovery, after which it was placed inside a column with a plaque that reads, 'Here rests the heart of Frédéric Chopin,' inscribed with the biblical adage, 'For where your treasure is, there your heart will be also.'"

Hazel studied him carefully, her curiosity piqued. "But you don't genuinely believe that, do you? From what I gather, you suspect the real heart, 'your treasure,' is still hidden here in the Maison."

His demeanour shifted as his eyes narrowed, a flicker of tension tracing through his shoulders. "And how do you deduce that?"

Hazel waved her hand dismissively at his question. "What truly matters is why you think the heart remains here."

Andre fell into a thoughtful silence for a moment, the weight of her inquiry apparent. "I've been researching Chopin's final days, and in my investigation, I believe I have uncovered his autopsy report, a document long thought to be lost. The existence of this report has been questioned for ages, leading many to doubt whether it ever existed at all. Until now, we had no evidence suggesting Chopin's heart was actually removed."

"Only the tale that his sister transported it to Warsaw?" Hazel pressed, eager for clarity.

Andre nodded affirmatively. "The claim that Chopin explicitly demanded his heart be sent to Poland lacks any substantial validity."

"So it was merely an act of devotion from his sister?" Hazel leaned forward, her interest intensifying. "Let's entertain the notion that his heart was removed during the autopsy—what makes you so certain it's hidden in Nohant?"

"That's a complex matter," he began, his brow furrowing in contemplation. "Chopin's father was French, and though Chopin lived in Paris, he never returned to Poland. At the time, there were questions about whether Chopin could even be considered Polish in the eyes of his countrymen."

"And?" Hazel encouraged, an edge of excitement in her voice.

"The Polish community believed otherwise. However, given that he was the lover of George Sand, it's conceivable that upon learning of Ludwika's intentions to move the relic, she decided to preserve his heart within her Maison, thus keeping him in France and sending a replica to Warsaw."

"So you're suggesting that George kept her lover's heart close? But can you substantiate such a claim?"

"Only by locating it," Andre responded, his expression earnest. "It could be anywhere within the depths of the Maison."

A sly smile crept onto Hazel's lips as a new thought crossed her mind. "It sounds like you ought to consult Obadiah."

Andre's expression darkened as he frowned. "That clumsy American? Why on earth would I do that?"

"He talks to ghosts," Hazel replied.

CHAPTER FORTY-TWO

Three individuals struck on the head. What were the odds of that happening in such a short span of time? Belinda pondered this unsettling thought as she handed a painkiller and a glass of water to Mrs. Alice, who sat on a plush chair, cradling her throbbing forehead with one hand. The incidents plagued Belinda's mind: one victim was dead, another had tumbled down a staircase, and now the well-known film producer lay injured. Could one person be behind all three attacks? Was the culprit someone from their group, or perhaps a villager? Belinda's imagination flared with vivid images of a deranged recidivist causing chaos—a dramatically unlikely scenario, she reminded herself, especially in this sleepy backwater of rural France. But still...

"Thank you, my dear," Mrs. Alice remarked gratefully, accepting the glass of water with shaky fingers. The other hand pressed a packet of frozen peas—stolen from the Priory kitchen—against her bruised forehead to quell the pain. "I was taken completely by surprise."

Belinda leaned closer, her curiosity piqued. "What were you doing in the Maison that would provoke such an attack?"

Mrs. Alice shot her a sharp glance, adjusting the peas with irritation. "Are you insinuating that I was engaged in something illegal?"

"Oh no, nothing like that," Belinda replied quickly, trying to soothe the older woman. "I'm just curious about what you might have seen or found that could have prompted your attacker to come after you."

Mrs. Alice hesitated, taking a sip from the glass and letting the cool water wash away some of her discomfort. "A secret? I was merely videoing the interior. I wanted a detailed record of the place—just a straightforward capture of each room as it exists."

Belinda's eyebrows arched. "Which room were you in when the attack occurred?"

"I believe it's called the theatre," Mrs. Alice replied, her brow furrowing as she recalled the ordeal. "It's not very impressive, mostly empty save for the small proscenium and stage."

"And you didn't see who attacked you?" Belinda pressed, a faint sense of urgency creeping into her tone.

"No," Mrs. Alice admitted, frustration evident in her voice. "I was preoccupied filming. I heard someone approach, and by the time I turned to look, I was struck. I fell and blacked out momentarily. When I came to, I was all alone."

"So you were filming as the attack happened? Was the camera still recording when you regained consciousness?"

Mrs. Alice pondered for a moment, her eyes narrowing in contemplation. "Yes, I think it was. I remember turning it off only after I got back on my feet. Why do you ask?"

"Because," Belinda said, "if the camera

was still running, it may have caught a glimpse of whoever assaulted you."

Dropping the peas, Mrs. Alice reached for her video camera, the small screen illuminating with a flicker of light. Both women leaned closer, watching intently as the image began to play. The video displayed the theatre, capturing the stark emptiness of the room with its faded drapes and dusty stage. But then, a sound echoed through the footage, and the camera swung around. A blurred figure emerged, raising an arm ominously before the picture jolted and fell to the ground, documenting only a shaky view of Mrs. Alice's feet as the recording persisted.

"Let's rewind to that figure and freeze the frame," Belinda instructed, urgency thickening her voice. Mrs. Alice did so, her fingers deftly navigating the controls until she paused on the blurry silhouette. "It's too indistinct to make out any features," Belinda murmured, disappointment lacing her tone. "But you were moving toward the side room. Was there something there you weren't meant to see?"

Rubbing her throbbing temple, Mrs. Alice considered, then replied cautiously, "On the other hand, I had been filming throughout the entire house. If there was something I was not supposed to witness, it could have been anywhere." Belinda frowned, contemplating the implications as Mrs. Alice, hoping to recover from the blow, slowly rose and retreated to her room. There could indeed be something concealed within the old Maison, but the group had had access for several weeks, and most rooms had been photographed and filmed numerous times. Why target Mrs. Alice specifically? To Belinda, it was clear: the attack stemmed from something Mrs. Alice had inadvertently stumbled upon.

"Well, the old girl has a point," Hazel said, as she and Belinda discussed the attack. After giving it due consideration, she added, "If someone had been tracking her and sensed she was close to uncovering whatever the secret is, they would have struck her elsewhere in the building. But the fact she was near the Marionettes suggests they are near to whatever must remain hidden."

Belinda nodded, her thoughts racing. "But what could it be? Just an innocent collection of dolls?"

Hazel adopted a self-assured posture, leaning back slightly. "Who knows? But let's not forget I caught ZeZe and Gino fiddling with the puppets that night."

Belinda's mind began swirling with possibilities. "And then there's Andre, who has been obsessed with finding Chopin's missing heart supposedly hidden somewhere in the house. Would he have attacked Mrs. Alice if he believed she was close to uncovering it?"

Hazel shook her head. "But there's the fly in that ointment—Andre was with me when the attack took place." Belinda weighed the options. "So, realistically, that leaves ZeZe, Gino, or possibly Jenny as suspects."

"Indeed," Hazel replied thoughtfully, "We can likely rule out Obadiah—he'd faint dead away at the thought of any violence."

"My instinct tells me we need to have a conversation with Jenny," Belinda concluded, a surge of determination propelling her forward. "I have a strong suspicion she's privy to some very dark secrets."

CHAPTER FORTY-THREE

Fortune smiled upon them as they stumbled upon Jenny, nestled in the greenery of the Priory garden, engrossed in her laptop. The soft rustling leaves provided a serene backdrop as Belinda wasted no time and approached Jenny with purpose. "The last time we spoke, you confirmed ZeZe was orchestrating this tour as a trial run for her ambitious plans to recreate a Nohant Village experience. Andre, on the other hand, is convinced that Chopin's heart is hidden within the Maison. So, where do you and Gino fit into all this?"

Jenny lifted her gaze from the screen, her expression a mixture of concern and resolve. "Quite frankly, I don't endorse what either of them is pursuing. ZeZe professes to be committed to upholding French history and traditions, yet she's manipulating her official position to conjure this farcical village setup. As a director of the company, she stands to profit immensely if it comes to fruition."

Hazel interjected, a frown creasing her brow, "So, you're suggesting she would go to any lengths to silence dissenting voices?"

Jenny offered a noncommittal shrug. "You could certainly interpret it that way."

Belinda pressed on. "And what about Andre? What drives him?"

"His conviction if the heart of Chopin in Warsaw is a mere imitation—while he possesses the real one—it would catapult him to hero status in his circle," Jenny explained, her voice pensive.

Belinda's eyes widened. "So, it appears they are both acutely aware of each other's ambitions."

Casting a cautious glance around the garden, Jenny confirmed, "Well, they were once married."

Hazel gasped in disbelief, "You must be joking!"

Jenny shook her head, her tone serious. "It was a significant scandal back in the day, with a lot of media frenzy surrounding it, especially since ZeZe is a prominent figure in the public eye. They divorced years ago, yet they've always seemed to be in a contest to one-up each other."

Belinda added thoughtfully, "And it appears they're still at it."

"Speaking of contests," Hazel said, her gaze sharp, "what about you and Gino?"

Belinda emphasized, "We know he's anything but mute and is indeed capable of speech. So why the charade?"

Jenny's expression darkened. "ZeZe is under the impression that he is working on her behalf. The ruse of being mute was meant to serve as a ploy—to gather intelligence on the tour guests, tapping into their private conversations and behaviours. What she doesn't realize is that Gino and I are married, and both of us are committed to stopping her plan." With a determined click, Jenny closed her laptop and hurried inside, leaving Belinda and Hazel amidst a whirlwind of thoughts and speculation. Hazel spoke up deliberately, her tone laced with intrigue, "Which brings us to an alarming conclusion: she had every motive to poison those chocolates."

Belinda nodded slowly, piecing it together. "Those chocolates were intended for ZeZe, but Joan ended up eating them after Gino inadvertently handed her the wrong envelope."

"Or so Jenny claims," Hazel interjected. Belinda scrutinized Hazel's expression, her brow furrowing. "You suspect she might be lying?"

"Someone is deceiving us," Hazel said steadily. "If Gino is truly playing the role of a double agent between ZeZe and Jenny, it raises troubling questions about where his true loyalties lie."

Belinda pondered the implications. "Are you suggesting he might have switched the envelope on purpose, perhaps to safeguard ZeZe?" The possibility hung uncomfortably in the air as the two women contemplated the tangled web of deception they found themselves enmeshed in.

CHAPTER FORTY-FOUR

"You've really found yourself mixed up with a right bunch of loonies," Macca remarked, shaking his head in disbelief as he adjusted the lens of his camera. The dying light of the afternoon streamed through the arched windows of the Church of Saint-Anne, casting intricate patterns of shadows over the ancient wall paintings that adorned its interior. The colours, though faded, still resonated with a sense of reverence that filled the sacred space with an otherworldly ambiance.

"Well, so have you," Belinda shot back with a wry smile. "You're working for ZeZe, after all."

Macca paused, lowering his camera as her words sank in. He met her gaze, a faint frown creasing his forehead. "Yeah, suppose you're right," he replied, his voice tinged with reluctant acknowledgment. A flicker of doubt formed in his eyes as he contemplated the implications of his association with ZeZe and the antics that surrounded him. With a resigned sigh, he resumed adjusting the lighting fixtures, intent on breathing life into the faded beauty of the murals. Belinda took this moment to step closer to the paintings, her fingertips lightly brushing against the cool plaster as she examined the delicate details. The last time she had been in this church, the atmosphere had been laden with foreboding, cloaked in the dim, shadowy glow of evening light. It was a night that had irrevocably altered the fabric of their lives; it was the night Mr. Henry was murdered—a crime that resonated like thunder throughout their small group. As she studied the intricate patterns and brushwork on the walls, her mind churned with thoughts of the recent crimes. "Do you think it *could* have been someone in our group?" she asked, her voice barely above a whisper, as if the very walls might overhear her and take offense. "Mr. Henry, Joan Smith, Mrs. Alice... Could they have been targeted for a specific reason?"

Macca rubbed the back of his neck, his brow furrowing deeper into thought. "Could there be *two* murderers?" he mused aloud, uncertainty creeping into his tone. He contemplated the tangled web the group had woven. Belinda pondered the possibility of a conspiracy, her mind racing to unravel any threads that could connect these grim events. And if there was a grand design behind it all, what could the purpose be? The familiar sound of the charabanc caught their attention. To their surprise it was driven by Andre and came to a stop at the gates of the Maison adjacent to the church.

From the shadows of the Maison, Obadiah emerged, his plump silhouette stark against the backdrop of the fiery sunset. He was met by Andre, who stood waiting by the charabanc, arms crossed, a serious expression etched deeply on his angular face. The sight surprised both Macca and Belinda, who exchanged glances filled with unspoken questions about this peculiar meeting between two men who, until now, had seemed to inhabit entirely different worlds. An undercurrent of intrigue ran through the air.

Obadiah's heart raced as he faced Andre, an imposing figure whose presence had always unsettled him. Memories of the embarrassing incident from earlier in their tour flooded his mind, amplifying his nervousness. Yet, to his astonishment, Andre wore a surprisingly friendly appearance, completely ignoring the awkwardness of their past encounters.

"Obadiah! How's the tour treating you now that you've rejoined us?" Andre's voice was warm, layered with genuine curiosity that disarmed Obadiah, even as anxiety twisted in his stomach. Unsure how to respond, Obadiah hesitated. After all, Andre had been prepared to confront him that night in the Maison. Did he still harbor those intentions? His fingers absently brushed against his bruised forehead as he took a small step backward, as if instinctively seeking distance. However, Andre appeared unfazed by their previous history, launching into light banter that dissolved the tensions of the past. Yet soon, the conversation shifted toward something that ignited Obadiah's interest. "I hear you have a fascinating device for communicating with spirits— or should I say, ghosts?"

At the mere mention of Frankie, Obadiah's initial shyness evaporated, replaced by an eager spark. He launched into an enthusiastic explanation of his methods for reaching out to the departed. His eyes brightened with passion, and as he produced the Spook Box, his previous unease faded into oblivion. With animated gestures, he described the thrill and nuances of contacting the dead. "I'm just about to head to the cemetery again," he declared eagerly. "It's the perfect setting, isn't it? A graveyard—a sacred space where earthly remains lie beneath the soil, making it the ideal place to bridge the gap between the living and those who have passed on." The logical reasoning behind his quest only fuelled the fervour of his words. To Andre, however, the Spook Box remained a mystery that he needed to see in action to echo Obadiah's undoubted enthusiasm.

"May I join you in your quest?" Andre asked, his brow slightly arching with interest. "Or would you rather be alone? Do the spirits avoid crowds?"

Obadiah let out a small, nervous giggle. "No! They love to have a chat." With a newfound confidence, he turned on his heel and now brimming with excitement began to lead the way toward the graves.

As the shadows deepened, Macca and Belinda, cautiously observing from the church's darkened recesses, felt a magnetic pull toward the unfolding mystery before them. With a blend of curiosity and trepidation, they stealthily moved from the church, navigating past the centuries-old tombstones and wrapping themselves in the thick foliage that bordered the graves. The setting sun had dipped below the horizon, draping the landscape in a veil of darkness that cloaked the world with an eerie stillness. From their hidden vantage point, they could make out the silhouettes of the two men who approached the graveyard—mere dark shapes against the twilight sky. Obadiah, the smaller of the two, exuded an aura of confidence, well-versed in the realm of the supernatural, as he held the Box before him in the manner of a Pectoral Cross.

The air was thick with anticipation as Andre's voice broke the silence, barely rising above a whisper. "What are you searching for?" His curiosity, palpable and intense, seemed to pierce through the darkness.

Obadiah met Andre's gaze with a look of solemn determination. "I want to make contact with Henry James, or Uncle James, as I call him," he replied, his eyes reflecting a mix of hope and gravity that suggested the weight of the task at hand. "This is about a family matter that requires resolution. Since James accompanied Edith Wharton on her original motor flight to Nohant, I'm hopeful that a spirit from that time can share vital information about Henry—information surrounding the web of relationships between him, Edith, and Morton Fullerton, her lover." Obadiah's speech drew Belinda and Macca deeper into a tapestry of speculation about the ghosts of the past.

Andre, leaning on a weathered gravestone that felt cold beneath his touch, raised an eyebrow sceptically. "If the Box really provides a link to the next world, I'll be impressed," he said, a hint of challenge in his voice. "I've tried using Ouija Boards in the past, but they've proven to be unreliable methods of communicating with the dead. However, I've found that automatic writing—where a spirit channels its energy through you, guiding your hand—tends to yield more profound results."

Obadiah's interest piqued at this revelation, but he turned his attention back to the task at hand. "You have a specific spirit you wish to contact?" Obadiah asked, adjusting the Spook Box—the curious device humming softly with latent energy—as he prepared it for use.

Andre hesitated. "Yes," he finally admitted. "I seek answers related to Chopin's death, which bear great significance to Poland and its history."

Obadiah's focus began to wane, the thrill of discovery momentarily overshadowed by the frustration of inaction. He waved the Box slowly across the silent graves, his voice a low murmur as he called out, "Is anybody there? Is there anyone willing to talk?"

A chilling breeze rustled the leaves overhead, as if mocking his efforts. For what felt like an eternity, only erratic static and a series of dissonant squeaks and shrieks emanated from the device, the spirits, it seemed, were preoccupied with their own affairs in that shadowy realm. After a painfully cold half hour, his hopeful demeanour cracked as disappointment settled in. "There must be something of importance happening on the other side," Obadiah sighed, frustration lacing his tone.

Although the night had yielded nothing of substance, a sense of determination swelled within Andre.

"I'll try in the Maison again," Obadiah muttered, glancing around the cemetery with uncertainty. Beside him, Andre was growing impatient. "It worked in the house?"

"Yes, ZeZe kindly let me in to see if I could get a response from any spirits there."

"And did you get one," said Andre anxiously.

"One or two odd words."

"What words?"

"Oh, a few that didn't mean anything to me," said Obadiah.

Gripping Obadiah's wrist with a strength that surprised them both, Andre said, "Try and remember."

"Er, something like 'body' and what was the other? Oh, 'alive'."

Andre sensed whoever used the spirit box held a certain power over it, a connection to the other realm that Obadiah seemed to lack. "Let's not waste time."

Obadiah's heart raced as the grip on his wrist tightened. He attempted to wrench his arm free, a wave of unease washing over him as he protested, "Let go of me!" But Andre, undeterred by Obadiah's discomfort, grinned grimly, "I think tonight is perfect for some serious ghost hunting," he said, practically dragging the reluctant man away from the cemetery and toward the Maison, their footsteps crunching on the gravel pathway.

Hidden just beyond the edge of the cemetery, Belinda and Macca, stunned by the unexpected turn of events, crept from their place of concealment. They stealthily followed the two men, their eyes fixed on the retreating figures, intrigued yet cautious as they speculated on what was to follow.

Grasping a reluctant Obadiah firmly by the scruff of his neck, Andre marched towards the imposing house that loomed before them. The wooden door creaked ominously as he pushed it open, revealing the interior thick with the scent of past centuries.

Belanda and Macca stopped. Opening the Citroën door he said, "Let's wait and see what happens next."

Andre and his prisoner stepped into the dimly lit Vestibule. Obadiah was shoved against the wall, his heart pounding with urgency. With a swift motion, Andre snatched the Spook Box from Obadiah's trembling hands, the weight of it solid and unfamiliar in his grasp. "Tell me how to make it work!" he demanded, his voice sharp and commanding. Obadiah, desperate and panicked, responded by trying to wriggle free from Andre's iron grip. But this only earned him a sharp blow to the head, sending a burst of pain shooting through him. "Tell me!" Andre shouted again, his tone brooking no argument. The impact knocked Obadiah's thin wire spectacles to the floor, and he blinked wildly, his eyes squinting in the dim light. Fear surged through him as he instinctively reached out, trembling fingers fumbling with the cold, intricate keys adorning the Box. Each key was a potential pathway to salvation, but the weight of Andre's threatening presence loomed large, and he couldn't shake off the thought that failure might result in another violent strike or something even worse from this mad man.

Enveloping the dimly lit room a sudden onslaught of erratic static crackled through the air. With a wild, instinctive movement, Andre's gaze darted around the space.

"Is there anyone there?" he called out, desperation lacing his voice.

In response to his plea, the room erupted into a bright flood of light, illuminating the corners and shadows as if some unseen force had orchestrated a grand theatrical display. The sudden luminosity transformed the atmosphere, elevating the strange encounter into something almost celestial.

Obadiah, now enabled by the brilliance around him, hastily searched the floor for his spectacles, his hands brushing against the cold floor. An unsatisfying crunch echoed in the stillness—he had located them. Unfortunately, one lens lay shattered beneath his foot, but the single remaining lens granted him a view of Andre, who was still fervently scanning his surroundings.

"I mean no harm," Andre spoke earnestly,

directing his words into the sweeping emptiness of the parlour. Dust motes hung lazily in the air, caught in the bright light, while framed portraits hung on the walls, their painted expressions a mix of haughtiness and curiosity. They seemed to observe him with bewilderment, as though pondering the presence of this night-time intruder, accompanied by the squawking of unseen creatures and half-formed whispers.

*** *Va t'en* ***

CHAPTER FORTY-FIVE

Emboldened by this unexpected spiritual acknowledgment, Andre felt a surge of determination course through him. His footsteps echoed purposefully on the floor as he made his way toward the Salle à Manger, each step infused with a sense of purpose.

"If you can hear me, please speak," he urged, his voice trembling with a mixture of trepidation and hope. To his astonishment, a faint, ghostly moan reverberated through the expansive room, the sound lingering in the air like a whisper from the beyond, igniting a spark of resolve within him.

"I need to speak to Frédéric Chopin. Is that possible?" he asked, his heartfelt question hanging heavily in the charged atmosphere. Suddenly, the silence shattered, giving way to a cacophony of static and the disjointed murmur of voices that drowned out all other sounds.

The lights above flickered ominously in response, casting eerie shadows that danced across the walls. Startled, Obadiah instinctively took a cautious step back, the hair on his arms standing on end as he sensed they were on the brink of a momentous connection—an ethereal encounter that would transcend the boundaries of life and death. The oppressive atmosphere thickened with anticipation, yet the room fell silent once more, offering no further signs of engagement.

Undeterred and driven by an unyielding

hope, Andre believed with all his heart that he could soon reach the essence of the great composer himself. He began to wander through the spaces of the house, his curiosity guiding him until he found himself standing before the door of the "des acteurs vivants", the grand theatre. A palpable feeling of destiny pulsed in his veins as he crossed the threshold, stepping into the mysterious realm that lay within.

"Fryderyk? I call you by your Polish baptismal name. Can you hear me?" he called out into the shadows of the room, the air thick with history and longing. "I know you wrote when you lay dying, 'As this earth will stifle me, I implore you to have my body opened, so I may not be buried alive.'" He paused, listening intently for any response amidst the uneven static that filled the air. Despite the silence, he remained resolute in his belief that he was reaching out to the spirit he sought. "Your heart was removed, and your sister took it to Warsaw. Or so we are told. I firmly believe your heart remains here in Nohant."

Again, silence enveloped him, yet Obadiah felt an icy chill descend upon the room, as if the very walls were holding their breath in anticipation of what might come next.

Clutching the Box, Andre began to wave it around the theatre, searching for any sign of a connection. "If I am correct, will you tell me where your heart is located?" he asked earnestly. Unexpectedly, a robotic voice filtered through the stillness, faint yet clear:

Mon Coeur...tu cherches?

A delighted smile illuminated Andre's face, dispelling his earlier fears. "Oui! Je cherche! I search. Tell me where it is hidden!" he exclaimed, his voice rising in excitement.

However, the response was drowned by an overwhelming wave of voices, each clamouring to be heard, all speaking over each other, further frustrating him as he desperately waved the Box in different directions, seeking to isolate the voice of Chopin amidst the chaos.

laissez-nous tranquille. qui êtes-vous ? Attention. éloignez-vous...

The clamour gradually faded to reveal a single voice cutting through the static, its tone commanding and urgent:

marionetka.

It took Andre a moment to realize the response had been in Polish. The word resonated with him, as he recognized it—'Marionette,' or 'Puppet'. Glancing at the theatre walls, he noticed a small proscenium arch, where a collection of marionettes stood frozen in mid-performance, their faces painted with an array of emotions. Could it be possible that the heart he sought was hidden amongst them? Another surge of static interrupted his thoughts, and the voice returned, more insistent than before:

non ! derrière toi

Andre spun around, his heart racing as

he caught sight of a small room just behind him. Without hesitation, he rushed toward it, his pulse quickening with each step. Inside, he discovered the table adorned with the eclectic collection of marionettes, their wooden limbs deftly crafted, grouped together as if engaged in a secretive conversation. Could the key to unlocking the heart of Frédéric Chopin lie within this enchanting tableau?

Obadiah stood at the doorway, his heart racing as he watched Andre make his way toward the table. The muted light of the room glinted off the assembly of puppets that encircled a central figure, their wooden faces carved with expressions of reverence and awe. Clad in ragged attire reminiscent of peasants and soldiers from a bygone era, they appeared to be both guarding and venerating the imposing puppet at the centre. This figure, draped in a dark cloak and adorned with a wide-brimmed hat, embodied an exaggerated embodiment of mid-nineteenth-century male fashion, a romanticized silhouette that loomed larger than life. As the stillness of the room settled like a heavy fog, the Box beside the puppets crackled ominously. A fractured voice emerged, echoing through the air before it faded into an unsettling silence.

C'est ça. Voici mon cœur.

The words hung in the atmosphere, charged with a cryptic significance. Andre's demeanour shifted; a triumphant sigh escaped his lips as he stood poised before his long-sought treasure. With a mixture of reverence and anticipation, he extended his hand, his fingers hovering over the dark fabric of the cloak before he finally mustered the courage to pull it away. What he unveiled wasn't a puppet at all, but rather an imposing cylindrical glass container. As he grasped the vessel, his fingers trembled, he slowly elevated it, as though presenting a sacred relic to an unseen congregation.

The glass shimmered dimly, revealing a dark liquid that swirled within, both alluring and foreboding. At the core of the container lay a grotesque, dark brown mass that seemed to pulse with a life of its own—the preserved tissue of a heart!

Stunned by the implications of his discovery, Andre's eyes widened with disbelief, and tears streamed down his cheeks, each droplet a testament to the weight of what he had found. A surge of exhilaration shot through him, and reality began to settle back into focus. In that moment, his thoughts turned frantic, driven by a singular desire—to flee with his precious find back to Warsaw, where he would be heralded as a hero for unveiling the heart of Chopin. The thought of adoring crowds celebrating his return filled him with adrenaline.

In his haste, he turned sharply, brushing past Obadiah, who had been watching with bated breath. It was only then that Obadiah's eyes fell upon the Box tightly clutched in Andre's grasp.

"My Spook Box! Frankie! Give him to me!" he shouted, the urgency in his voice rising as he realized what was happening.

But Andre was already racing from the Vestibule. Panic surged through Obadiah, propelling him to follow, calling out for Frankie's release. As he burst through the front door into the night, he barely registered the dark shape lurking ominously on the stairs, a figure that seemed to blend effortlessly with the shadows. The sound of laughter—a triumphant, malicious laugh—echoed behind him, reverberating through the stillness and heightening the tension of the moment.

CHAPTER FORTY-SIX

As the frigid air seeped into the cabin of the Citroën, Macca turned the key in the ignition with a resigned sigh. Both he and Belinda had come to the mutual conclusion that their mission was proving futile, and the biting cold was quickly becoming unbearable. Just as the engine sputtered to life, the door of the Maison opened, and Andre emerged in a flurry of movement. He darted towards the charabanc, a sense of urgency propelling him forward. With an almost frantic determination, he scrambled into the driver's seat, his hands swiftly gripping the steering wheel as he shifted the car into motion.

The vehicle lurched forward, tires crunching against the gravel driveway, but before it had covered more than a few feet, a sudden commotion erupted behind them. Obadiah, his face flushed with exertion and alarm, burst out of the house and sprinted towards the charabanc. His short legs pumped furiously as he drew closer to the car, the cold air filling his lungs. With a desperate reach, he yanked open the door and, in a swift motion, hauled himself aboard just as the charabanc picked up speed.

"Give back Frankie!" he wailed breathlessly.

Belinda and Macca, momentarily taken aback by the unexpected scene unfolding before them, exchanged startled glances. Intrigued by the unfolding drama, they instinctively followed, their hearts racing as they sought to understand the sudden desperation of both men. What could have driven them to such urgent action?

Both vehicles tore through the village with reckless abandon, their engines roaring like angry beasts. The cacophony startled some villagers, prompting them to peer cautiously from their doorways, while others hurriedly bolted their windows against the commotion.

The night was an inky blackness, punctuated only by the glaring beams of their headlights, as the tense chase surged into open fields, stretching into an abyss of shadows. Inside the lead car, Andre wrestled with Obadiah, whose fists rained down like a storm, each blow accompanied by frantic attempts to reach the vulnerable Frankie. The charabanc swerved perilously off the road, its tires kicking up dust and gravel. Andre's mind was a whirlwind, with no clear destination guiding him, save for the desperate hope of reaching a community that would lead him safely back home to Warsaw. The precious container, housing that revered heart, nestled tightly against his side, seemed to pulse with an otherworldly strength, empowering him to navigate the treacherous terrain ahead.

Behind them, Macca and Belinda clung onto the ancient Citroën, its frame a testament to years of weathering the elements. With every jolting bump and sharp turn, they prayed it would hold together, resisting the urge to surrender to the strain of high-speed pursuit. Their eyes, fixed intently on the distant charabanc, widened in unease as a flickering light appeared on the dark road ahead. Was it another vehicle?

As Andre turned once more to fend off Obadiah's grasp, the desperation of the moment intensified. Obadiah lunged for Frankie, and in that split second of distraction, Andre's grip on the wheel faltered. A strange object ahead loomed larger, its form looming ominously as it raced toward them through the shadows.

Andre jolted in his seat, his breath quickening as he fought off Obadiah's desperate hands, trying to push him aside for the sake of safety. With his focus veering back to the winding road ahead, he squinted into the distance, only to see the ominous shape hurtling toward them—a strange object that sent a chill creeping down his spine. In a moment of distraction, as he let Frankie slip free from his grip.

Obadiah's eyes widened in horror as he registered the impending danger at the same moment. Panic surged through him, and he fumbled with the door handle, his fingers stiff and trembling, nearly paralysed by fear. The unmistakable, acrid scent that accompanied the massive oncoming vehicle filled the air—an all-too-familiar aroma to him, heralding the approach of a farm tractor. The thunderous roar of its engine rumbled like a warning, echoing through the narrow lane.

Realizing the gravity of the situation too late, Andre swerved desperately, trying to dodge the relentless beast barrelling down upon them. But it was no use; a farmer's tractor, pulling a hefty trailer overflowing with manure, was a force of nature that could not be avoided. With a sickening crunch, the charabanc collided with the rear of the trailer, the impact reverberating through the metal frame of the vehicle. Time seemed to slow as Andre was propelled forward, his body hurled headfirst through the shattered windscreen, shards of glass glinting like deadly confetti in the night. The shattered glass severing an artery.

Obadiah and Frankie, caught in the chaos, tumbled from the vehicle, landing in a vile torrent of manure, hay, and decaying fruit, a nauseating mix that enveloped them almost instantly. In the frenzy of the crash, the precious glass container filled with its dark and mysterious content flew upward, then shattering upon impact on a jagged rock, sending its contents—a thick, brown fluid—splattering onto the ground, mingling grotesquely with the manure.

As the headlights of the crushed charabanc cast eerie beams onto the scene, a grotesquely distorted brown shape lay exposed in the chaos, a silent testament to the chaos that had just unfolded.

CHAPTER FORTY-SEVEN

"I guess it's my fault," Hazel admitted, her voice barely above a whisper. Belinda and Obadiah turned to look at her, their brows furrowed in interest. "Why do you say that?" Belinda pressed, her tone both curious and comforting.

Hazel shrugged, a motion that seemed to carry the weight of regret. "I told Andre he should meet with Obadiah because he spoke to ghosts. I thought I was being funny, but it seems he took it seriously. I never imagined someone as intelligent as him would actually believe me."

Her gaze fell on the Queen Eleanor Memorial Cross in the Strand, a poignant reminder of their earlier visit—a time that now felt like a distant memory. Just weeks ago, she had stood there with an air of innocence, enjoying the sights of London from the hotel suite. Now, that same suite seemed shrouded with the dark shadows tainted by the haunting memories of three people whose lives had been lost in the chaos.

Obadiah, a wave of cologne masking the imagined stench of manure only he could smell, placed his coffee cup down carefully on the table. "I don't think you can blame yourself for Andre's death," he said, his voice firm yet gentle.

Hazel caught his eye, intrigued by this peculiar little American who had unexpectedly entered their lives.

Macca entered the hotel suite, bearing a

copy of The Times and Le Monde. "Well, the hounds of Fleet Street have got into ZeZe!"

He handed the papers to Belinda and Hazel, who began devouring the scandal. "Jenny spilled her guts to the media about ZeZe's plans to commercialise Nohant village all the time pretending to preserve France's history safe from exploitation, and she's persona non grata. Gone into hiding."

"And Jenny has been charged with murder?" said Belinda.

"Yeah," said Macca sinking into a comfy chair and pouring a beer. "Murder of Joan and attempted murder of ZeZe. Gino charged as an accessory." He turned to Obadiah, "What are your plans now?"

With a glimmer of enthusiasm, Obadiah replied, "I'm scheduled to travel to Rye in East Sussex to visit Lamb House, which is where Uncle Henry lived." He waved a package in the air, almost like a trophy. "I've got a brand-new super Spook Box. It's far superior to the previous one. I've named this one 'Francis'" he added with a hint of pride.

Belinda, intrigued said, "Do you expect to make contact with your uncle there?"

Obadiah sank back into thoughtful contemplation. "Well, I can certainly try. He used to write in the Garden Room during the summer months, but that was utterly destroyed by a German bomb during the war." His expression shifted to one of uncertainty, but he quickly covered it with a cheerful smile. "I believe his spirit still lingers in the

House, and I'll definitely reach out."

Macca leaned forward, intrigued. "What exactly do you expect to learn from him?"

Obadiah suddenly looked bashful, his confidence wavering. "Well, it's a bit of a family matter. It pertains to him and Merton Fullerton. I suspect there might be a connection..." His voice trailed off, and he retreated back into his usual timid self.

"What were you doing at the Maison that night?" Macca said, redirecting the conversation.

Obadiah brightened as he recalled the encounter. "It was quite strange, really. Out of nowhere, ZeZe wanted to meet me. She'd heard about Frankie and was curious to learn how it operated and how it contacted spirits. We decided to meet at the Maison, and I began to make some attempts. She seemed eager to understand how the voices sounded. But, our results were mostly static and a few half-spoken words that felt unusual. It could have been because we were indoors, but she seemed satisfied, nonetheless. I suggested trying again in the cemetery, but she said no. So, I went out alone, and that's when I ran into Andre."

Belinda's expression turned contemplative. "So, she was investigating how the voices worked?"

"Seems so," Macca agreed, the pieces of the puzzle beginning to fit together. "The police found the speaker she'd hidden in the theatre. And it was Gino upstairs with a microphone, creating the ghostly directions for Andre to find the heart."

"Humph," Hazel interjected, her disbelief evident. "Some heart. A dried-up old sheep's ticker. Three dollars at the butchers."

Macca chuckled. "Precisely what ZiZi hoped to reveal when Andre returned to Warsaw, claiming it was Chopin's, whereas if you add anchovy, garlic, and rosemary, you've got Sunday lunch..."

"I'm impressed," said Belinda, "a Chef as well as a photographer."

Macca acknowledged the comment with a thumbs up. "He would have been ridiculed. From what I can gather Andre heard of ZeZe's plan to convert Nohant into a money-making machine and wanted part of it. He conceived the idea that Chopin's heart was in the Maison and if he proved it, he would hold ZeZe to ransom and be her business partner."

"Seems he wasn't much good as a marriage partner, " said Hazel.

"True, and ZeZe wanted nothing to do with him," said Macca, "but hearing about Obadiah and Frankie, she thought of a scheme to use them to ensure Andre found a heart and make him the laughingstock of Poland."

"A woman scorned," Belinda muttered, "Plus, it meant her ambitions for Nohant remained unharmed."

"And what of Gino," said Hazel as she searched the pages of the newspaper.

"Complicated," said Macca, "seems although he was married to Jenny, ZeZe made him an offer he couldn't refuse. He kept her informed as to how the group was reacting to the tour, including Jenny, and when he learned she opposed ZeZe's development plans, this was passed on. Gino bought the poison for Jenny and knew of her plan, but he was in ZeZe's pay all the time and couldn't kill a Golden Goose."

"Which means, as we suspected, he swapped the letter on purpose, so that ZeZe would not be poisoned. Joan, it seems, was disposable," said Belinda.

"Gino. Charming creature," said Hazel.

Belinda gave a nod in agreement. "I think he's the one who hit Mrs. Alice on the head to prevent her from getting too close to the fake heart which was disguised as a puppet."

Macca glanced at his watch, the reality of time weighing on them. "You'd better get going if you want to catch the train to Bath," he said, as he turned to Belinda. "I've never been to Bath. Perhaps I should tag along."

Belinda's face lit up. "Why not? I'm sure we can fit you in. You can do the cooking!" As they gathered their bags, Hazel took a final sip of her gin and tonic. "Well, we're all on our way then. I can't help but wonder how Mrs. Alice is faring back in Hollywood?"

. . . .

Mrs. Alice carefully set the suitcase on the plush, inviting bed in her elegant Beverly Hills home. "I

184

must say, Maria, you have done an exceptional job keeping the place immaculate during my absence. It looks flawless," she remarked, her voice warm with appreciation but tinged with distraction. "This is the last case. Would you be a dear and deal with it? It's the one I took when I had to go to hospital. Now I have some contracts that demand my attention." With that, she began sifting through a stack of envelopes, their contents seemingly urgent.

Maria, her dedicated housekeeper, opened the case letting a mix of clothing and toiletries spill out. "It's truly wonderful to have you back home, Madam," Maria said softly, her voice filled with a hint of melancholy. "But this homecoming is shadowed by such sadness, especially without Mr. Henry after that dreadful incident. Are you still planning to continue with your new film project in France? It will be challenging without him by your side."

Mrs. Alice barely glanced up from the envelope she was intent on tearing open. "I'm quite certain I can manage the production entirely on my own, Maria," she replied, her tone resolute but distracted. Her gaze drifted down to the floor, where a cardboard box sat innocuously. With a swift, practiced movement, she nudged it beneath the bed, hiding it from view. "I don't require any assistance."

Maria's eyes widened in concern as she inspected the suitcase more closely. "Madam, this suitcase appears to be damaged," she exclaimed, an edge of alarm creeping into her voice. "Your new Louis

Vuitton... oh my!"

"Mmm?" Mrs. Alice responded, distractedly, her preoccupation with the contract showing no signs of waning.

"The lining inside has been torn, and there's something pressed down behind it!" Maria's fingers worked diligently to free the hidden object, her brows furrowed in concentration. After a few moments of persistent struggle, she managed to extract it and bring it into the light.

"Why, Madam, it's a glove!" she announced, holding up a black leather item with both surprise and sadness. "The ones Mr. Henry gifted you for your birthday. But look—it's just the left glove!" She returned to the suitcase, her hands searching frantically through the torn lining for any sign of its mate, but her efforts were in vain.

"Madam, it appears that only the left-hand glove remains. The right one is missing!"

Mrs. Alice finally lifted her gaze from the contract, her expression one of mild concern that quickly faded back into practised indifference.

"Oh dear," she murmured, her voice barely rising above a whisper. "I must be getting careless!"